The Black Glass City

Also by Judson Philips

THE LAUGHTER TRAP
(*A Peter Styles Mystery*)

THE DEAD CAN'T LOVE

A DEAD ENDING

MURDER CLEAR, TRACK FAST

WHISPER TOWN

KILLER ON THE CATWALK

THE FOURTEENTH TRUMP

ODDS ON THE HOT SEAT

MURDER IN MARBLE

The Black Glass City

A PETER STYLES MYSTERY

By Judson Philips

DODD, MEAD & COMPANY

New York

RED BADGE

DETECTIVE

Library of Congress Catalog Card Number: 65-11808

Printed in the United States of America
by Vail-Ballou Press, Inc., Binghamton, N. Y.

Part One

1

"I WISH YOU'D stop looking at me as if I were a movie star," Carol Richmond said.

It was an odd request, because she was certainly the top luminary in the present-day Hollywood constellation.

Peter Styles grinned at her. "If you'd take off your shoes and those black glasses, I might give it a try," he said.

She didn't answer. The black glasses moved slowly around the living room of Peter's Gramercy Park apartment—along the bookshelves that lined the side walls, to the French doors that opened out onto a small garden, to the red coals in the fireplace, to the big flat-topped desk in the center of the room with a droplight hanging over the center of it, illuminating disorder. Then the glasses came back to Peter himself, studied his dark, handsome face for a moment, twisted slightly by a mocking smile, and then slowly, hesitantly, down toward the long legs stretched out in front of him.

Peter took the black shell-briar pipe out of his mouth, reached down, and tapped his right shin bone with the bowl, There was a curious, hollow sound.

"It's this one," he said, casually. "Plastic, with some mysterious springs and hinges that make it almost as efficient as the original."

"Oh, Peter!"

"I find it easier to talk about it at once with old friends who haven't seen me since it happened," Peter said. He held his lighter to the bowl of his pipe. "It gets the embarrassment and the faint cluckings of sympathy over with in a hurry."

"I was in Greece, making a picture, when it happened," Carol said. "We didn't see any American newspapers. I didn't hear about it until months afterwards. Then—"

"Then, since you hadn't seen me or communicated with me for more than twenty years, there didn't seem any reason to do so then." Peter's smile widened. "You were also very busy with—is it husband number four?"

"Yes," she said in a flat voice. "Francis and I were married in Greece."

"Francis—? I'm sorry, but the full handle escapes me."

"Francis X. Garrity," she said. "I am Mrs. Francis X. Garrity."

"Then I'll try to look at you as though you were Mrs. Garrity," Peter said.

"Does it—is it too painful to tell me how it happened, Peter?"

"The leg?" His straight, firm mouth hardened. "My father and I were driving down a mountain road in Vermont from a ski lodge where we'd been week-ending. Two lunatic young men began to play games with us, passing and repassing us—laughing at us, calling us 'chicken'! It was some kind of game—for kicks. They'd pass us, go ahead, pull off on a side road and let us get ahead, and then demand to pass us again—so close they scraped our fenders. My father—my father lost his nerve and grabbed the wheel. We went through the guardrail and somersaulted down a five-hundred-foot embankment into the valley below. I was thrown clear." Peter's pipe had gone out, but he did't notice. He drew a deep breath. "My father was burned to death in the wreckage. I—well, my right leg was so badly smashed it had to be amputated below the knee. The two young men responsible were never caught. 'Joy-killers' the police called them. When I'd recovered from the shock and learned to use my new foot, I began to look for them. I've never found them. But if you've been reading my articles in *Newsview,* you know that I found myself embarked on a sort of crusade—fighting the state of mind that seems to have engulfed us as a nation. Don't care-ism. Ignore those who practice violence for kicks. Let someone else handle the juveniles who knife their teachers in the public schools of New York. Ignore the climate of hate and bigotry that could lead to the assassination of a President, to the murder of children in a Birmingham church, to vandalism, and irresponsible slander, and God knows what else." He grinned at his caller. "Sorry, I didn't mean to embark on a lecture. About the leg. I felt mutilated and crippled and an object of pity when it happened. Thank the Lord that's behind me. I had a seventy-eight at Winged Foot yesterday. My golf wasn't any better than that before the accident. If you'll go out with me some evening, I'll demonstrate to you that I can dance quite acceptably. It's no obstacle to a perfectly normal life."

Carol moistened her bright red lips. "How—how do women react to it?"

Peter grinned. "That, my darling, is none of your business." He put his pipe down in an ash tray on the table beside his chair. "Seriously, I'd like it if you'd take off your glasses."

Very slowly Carol Richmond reached up and took off the black-lensed glasses and dropped them in her lap. He sat in silence for a moment, staring at the beautiful face, the curious excitement in the depths of dark violet eyes.

"The last time I saw you in the flesh," Peter said, "was exactly twenty-one years ago last fall. I was fifteen and you were fourteen. Do you remember it?"

She turned her eyes away, as though remembering was an effort.

"I was due to go off to school the next day," Peter said. "You were the girl next door. We were friends—just friends. I used to take you fishing sometimes when there weren't any boys to go with. I took you that last morning. It was early. Six o'clock. I brought some sandwiches and a thermos of milk in a lunch box. You wore blue jeans and a loose-fitting boy's shirt. You were barefoot. Your hair was gold in the early morning sun. I could even tell you the color of your father's necktie which you were wearing as a belt."

"I don't know how you remember all that," she said without looking at him.

"The sandwiches were cold ham for me and raspberry jelly for you. We fished awhile and were very quickly hungry. We sat down on the bank of the stream and ate our sandwiches. Somehow—maybe while I was passing you a sandwich—I touched your hand. Something happened to me that had never happened before at age fifteen. It was like electricity running through me from head to foot. We stared at each other, because you'd felt it too. And then—then I kissed you." He laughed softly. "In that moment I stopped being an adolescent and became a man. You were all I wanted in the whole world—for the rest of time."

"But you got over it," she said, still not looking at him.

"I got over it," he said, "but not right away. I knew I had to get educated, to learn to make a living, to be in a position to tell you what I felt as quickly as possible. My one aim in life was to reach the point where I could ask you to marry me. It stayed my aim for quite a while, Carol, even though I didn't see you again, and after six months you stopped answering my letters. Your family moved away, you remember, across the country to Hollywood. At sixteen you were in pictures. At eighteen you were married. That shook me a little, because I was just a sophomore in college. But I still had the notion that somehow, when I was ready, you'd be waiting for me. But—when I was ready, my sweet, you had just taken on your second husband at age twenty. And I'd really grown up and realized it was time to abandon fantasy."

"And since then," she said bitterly, "I've acquired my fourth husband and have a series of highly publicized affairs behind me. You were lucky, Peter. Some people have problems with alcohol or dope. Mine has always been men."

"If the gossip columns are to be believed, husband number five has already appeared on the scene," Peter said not too gently.

"No!"

He looked at her steadily. "Twenty-one years—and then on a pleasant fall evening you ring my doorbell," he said.

"It was just a whim," she said. "You're a famous writer, Peter. I've always read your articles. I've thought about you often. Then I—well, I just happened to come across your name in the phone book. Impulse made me ring your doorbell."

"I don't think so," Peter said.

The dark violet eyes turned on him.

"You came for help," he said. "Something's frightening you out of your wits, Carol. Shall we stop playing games? I'll help if I can."

A nerve twitched high up on her cheek, and then she covered her lovely face with her hands and began to weep.

Peter got up from his chair and moved across the room to the sideboard. Only someone who knew would have detected the imperceptible hesitation in his walk. He poured some brandy in a glass and brought it back to Carol.

"I feel so close to you," he said, "and yet I don't know your drinking habits. You didn't have any the last time I saw you. Try this Martel."

She took the glass in an unsteady hand and drained it.

"I'm sorry," she said, "I'm all right now." The tear-stained eyes somehow made her look much younger, much less sophisticated. "Someone is trying to destroy me, Peter, as an actress and as a person."

"Before you tell me about it," Peter said, "I'd like to ask you a question. Francis X. Garrity you said his name is? Your husband? Why aren't you asking him for help? Why me?"

"Because," Carol said in a low voice, "Francis may be my enemy."

The doorbell rang.

Peter made a little gesture of impatience. "Excuse me a minute," he said. He went out of the living room and into the little foyer and opened the front door. The man who confronted him was a complete stranger. He was in his fifties, Peter thought. He wore a beautifully tailored dinner jacket. He was bald, and heavy shell-rimmed glasses gave him an owlish look.

"Peter Styles?" he asked, with a polite little bow.

"Yes."

"My name is Francis X. Garrity," the man said. "I believe my wife is visiting you."

Peter heard a little gasp of surprise from the room behind him. He shrugged his broad shoulders. "Come in, Mr. Garrity," he said.

Peter stood aside to let this unexpected guest go past him

into the living room. Carol was out of her chair, standing with her back to Peter's desk, her hands gripping the edge behind her. The black glasses once more hid the deep, smoldering eyes.

"You had me followed, Francis!" she said sharply.

It was a chill fall evening, but Mr. Francis X. Garrity was wearing neither hat nor coat. Probably in a waiting car outside, Peter thought. He was slim, elegant in his manner, and his voice had a gentle, soothing quality to it, simulated or for real, Peter couldn't tell.

"Of course I had you followed, my darling," he said, as though it was the most natural thing in the world. He turned to Peter, and his thin lips moved in a wry little smile. "Please don't get the notion, Mr. Styles, that I represent the jealous husband on the warpath."

"You had me followed!" Carol's voice was shrill.

"My charming wife is blithely unaware of the fact that she just can't go places alone without running the risks of embarrassment—in the form of mob scenes—and possibly real danger. The price one pays for being so glamorously in the public eye. I do have her watched, for her own safety."

"And so there were no mob scenes and no trouble and I came to see an old friend—and you had me followed!"

"We are always in jeopardy, Mr. Styles," Garrity said. "There is danger of kidnaping. There is danger of blackmailing. When my wife goes into a strange neighborhood for her, and into a strange house, there is always the distinct possibility that she may have been forced to go there against her will. To protect herself or me." The gentle smile widened. "I can't tell you how relieved I was when I saw your name on the brass plate outside, Mr. Styles. You see, I know that you were a childhood friend of Carol's. She mentioned it one day when I'd read one of your articles in *Newsview* to her."

"As a matter of fact, Carol and I haven't seen or communicated with each other for roughly twenty years," Peter said.

"Childhood friends are often less remote than present-day connections," Garrity said.

The black glasses flashed Peter's way for an instant. "I was having tea at the Cosmopolitan Club," Carol said. "I was reading *Variety* and I saw that Jane Cooper was in town from Hollywood, staying at the St. Moritz. I was looking up the number in the phone book when I came across Peter's name. On impulse I called him and he invited me down here for a drink."

Lie number one, Peter thought.

"It must have been fun to meet again," Garrity said. "I regret to remind you, darling, that you must be back at Marlingham and ready to get started at five in the morning. Marshall is waiting outside in the car for us."

Peter thought there was a kind of tense despair in Carol's manner as she moved across the room for the mink coat she'd left on the bench by the door.

"Please consider yourself most welcome in our rather complex lives, Mr. Styles," Garrity said, watching his wife. "We'll probably be at Marlingham for another six months. If you'd like to come up sometime and see how Monty Spain shoots one of his epics, you'll be most welcome. The golf is still good, and if you care for riding, there's a wonderful string of horses. Both a little too vigorous for me, I'm afraid. But we could find you company, couldn't we, darling?"

The black glasses leveled straight at Peter. "Please come," Carol said in a low, almost breathless voice. Then she held out her hand to Peter. "It's been wonderful seeing you again." It was a completely formal mannered good-by.

Peter took the cold hand in his, but he spoke to Garrity.

"Your wife and I used to go fishing together when we were kids."

The owlish eyes turned blandly to Peter. "From what I read about you, Mr. Styles, a kind of fishing is still your chief interest in life. It must be interesting to spend your life on the trail of meaningless and heartless violence. So satisfying when you come up with a fish you don't have to throw back." He gave Peter a small bow. "Thank you for taking such good care of my wife. Good night, sir."

2

THERE WAS no doubt in Peter Styles' mind that the fear of something Carol Richmond hadn't gotten to tell him about was very real. The unwelcome appearance of her husband had shut her off just as she'd been about to tell him. "Francis may be my enemy," were the last words she's spoken before the doorbell rang. Garrity could well be a dangerous enemy, Peter thought. Underneath that suave, gentle exterior was a hard core of something as yet undefined.

It was only about eight o'clock in the evening when the Garritys left Peter's apartment. Peter took a chance, knowing that Bill Tompkins, the movie critic of *Newsview,* often spent his evenings at the Players Club, which was just around the corner from the apartment. His luck was in. Tompkins was seated at a small round table in the bar at the Club just finishing a late dinner. He welcomed Peter cordially, the Club being somewhat deserted at the moment.

"Lot of guys upstairs playing poker, but nobody to talk to," Tompkins said. "Sit down and charm me. Buy you a drink?"

"No, thanks," Peter said, sitting down under Gordon Stevenson's charming portrait of Mark Twain. "Matter of fact I came here to find you—and pump you."

"Pump away," Tompkins said, signaling to Juan, the bartender, to refill his highball glass.

"Who," Peter asked, slowly filling his pipe, "is Francis X. Garrity?'

"Carol Richmond's latest husband," Tompkins said promptly. "Said to be confronted by a new pretender to the throne."

"But who is he?"

"Soft drinks," Tompkins said. "Low-calorie soft drinks. Dieting America has made him a millionaire."

"What else?"

Tompkins laughed. "You might call him a surprise package. The last man in the world anyone would have thought of as Carol Richmond's husband. Only answer is she'd suddenly become obsessed with a father-image. And from all accounts is just about over the disease and will shortly be hailing number five, in the person of the explosive Mark Fleming, this year's answer to Clark Gable and Richard Burton."

"Carol and I were kids together," Peter said.

"Don't tell me you were the first!" Tompkins exclaimed gleefully.

"Down, boy," Peter said. "At fifteen you reverence the women you love." He held his lighter to his pipe, "Where and what is Marlingham?"

"I'm hurt. Deeply, deeply hurt," Tompkins said, his eyes twinkling.

"Why?"

"I just did a feature on Marlingham for our mutual editor," Tompkins said. "I read your stuff, old boy. The least you could do—"

"I apologize," Peter said. "Do me a brief recap."

Tompkins leaned back in his chair and lit a cigarette.

The subject, obviously, didn't bore him. "Brief may not be easy," he said. "Marlingham is a fabulous private estate in northwest Connecticut. Foothills of the Berkshires. It was built by a man named Leonard Moffet on profits from the Civil War. Cotton mills. Uniforms, I suppose. It is a forty-room house sitting high on a hill, surrounded by hundreds and hundreds of acres of cultivated land. Moffets down through the years have kept pace with everything modern, including air conditioning, an elevator, and half a dozen Picassos among other art treasures. There's a stable for fifty horses, built in the days when horses were the means of transportation. When cars came in at the turn of the century, a twelve-car garage with its own machine shop was added. Moffets turned to raising and training the best jumpers and steeplechase horses in America. Along the way one of the Moffets built himself a private eighteen-hole golf course. There are two swimming pools, one natural and one with temperature-controlled water—Olympic dimensions. Physically, that's Marlingham."

"I didn't know such places existed any more."

"Marlingham is just holding on by its teeth," Tompkins said. "In 1960 the last Leonard Moffet died, leaving a childless widow, Clarissa Moffet. The funeral was magnificent. There was a message of condolence from the President. A Senator delivered the eulogy. The governors of three states were among the honorary pallbearers. It was on television, which I take it you're too high-toned to watch."

"I've looked at television once this year," Peter said. "The Beatles."

"God help us all," Tompkins said. He took a swallow of his drink. "A few days after the funeral Mrs. Clarissa Moffet got the bad news from the lawyers. Her husband had been living on capital for the last fifteen years. The L. P. Moffet Company is now a rival of DuPont in the manufacture of modern plastics. But the last of the Moffets had long since ceased to have any sort of control of the company. He did leave Clarissa about two hundred and fifty thousand bucks —and fabulous Marlingham. You and I would think ourselves well off. We'd hastily sell the property and spend the rest of our lives doing exactly what we pleased on the income from a million bucks. Not Clarissa. She's a doll, by the way. Old-world elegance spiced with a delightful modern sense of humor. But no sense of money, I gather. Nobody could or would buy Marlingham in one piece. A man interested in raising Thoroughbreds offered a fancy price for the stables and the property that goes with them, including a famous trial course for jumpers. No dice. A local group offered to buy the golf course to start a private club. Again no dice. It costs a good fifty thousand a year to keep up the grounds and the golf course. Clarissa's quarter million can't go very far. But she has refused flatly to sell the place piecemeal. She's been living in the house by herself with one maid-of-all-work, most of the antiques and paintings under dust covers, paying the salaries of a twelve-man crew that keeps the grounds immaculate."

"So she's close to the end of her tether," Peter said.

"She was," Tompkins said. "Which is where the motion picture critic of *Newsview* magazine comes into the picture. Sure you won't have a drink?"

"I'll buy," Peter said. "That's the least I can do."

Juan was summoned to supply drinks. Someone stopped at the table to pass the time of day. Eventually Tompkins got back to his story with a question.

"Have you ever met Montague Spain?"

"No," Peter said. "I've seen pictures of him. I know he's the top producer-director in pictures today."

"That barely scratches the surface," Tompkins said. "Physically he is, to say the least, eye-catching. An oversized mountain. Three hundred pounds; grizzled brown hair and beard; diamond-hard blue eyes that look out at you from behind hooded lids and seem to be reading the maker's name on the inside of your shirt collar. Basically a cruel man. I can imagine him as a fat little boy sitting in a sunny window somewhere, pulling the wings off flies and giggling."

"Sounds charming."

"Not charming—but arresting," Tompkins said, frowning slightly. "There's a fierce energy inside him that burns with blowtorch heat. It holds you. It fascinates you. He's a pro in his field; a real pro. He squanders money, and yet his pictures always show a big profit. In a period of twenty years he's made at least half a dozen really memorable pictures and a great many very good ones. People who use the word lightly call him a genius. I have called him a pro, which is the highest compliment I know how to pay him. But—"

"There's always a 'but,' " Peter said. "Ask about anyone and there's always a 'but.' "

"The 'buts' always come about for the same reason," Tompkins said. "Is what you get worth the price you pay for it? Monty Spain is at his brilliant best when everyone around him has been reduced to screaming hysteria, are at each other's throats, and are, at the same time, quaking with fear of him. In his world he has the power of life and death, the ability to make or break careers. He's been quoted as saying that a calm actor never gives you a high-powered performance. He carries this theory far beyond his cast of actors. A calm camera crew can't do a high-powered job, nor can a calm costume designer, or makeup man, or sound technician, or art director, or script girl, or chef in the commissary. Or, for that matter, the members of the press brought there by his public relations crew to keep his production in the public eye before it's released. Everyone's nerves must be filed down to an unendurable rawness before Monty Spain is at his best. Behind his back they call him The Monster. It fits."

"He's directing Carol Richmond's current picture?"

"At Marlingham," Tompkins said, lighting a fresh cigarette. "Some months ago The Monster conceived the idea of doing a feature film which he blandly announced would be 'a modern morality play.' The story, he admitted freely, had been suggested by D. H. Lawrence's *Lady Chatterley's Lover*. I've read the script. The bones of the story involve the wife of an incredibly rich sportsman whose hobby is horses, and her affair with a monumental sex symbol in the person of a man the husband has hired to act as a trainer for him. Now long before there was even the beginning of a shooting script, The Monster announced that the leads would be played by the four-times married and God knows how many times loved Carol Richmond and Mark Fleming, Hollywood's top he-man.

"Such a move is a part of the economics of modern movie making. They say the star system is dead, but only star names are bankable today. Banks don't dare rely on talent, which is why our young hopefuls are flocking to Europe these days to make pictures. Banks can't read scripts. So they put their money on the 'chemistry' of star combinations. The mixture of Carol Richmond and Mark Fleming under the diabolical guidance of Montague Spain is money in the bank. About eight million dollars, in this case."

"A pretty explosive combination," Peter said.

"Explosive!" Tompkins laughed. "Just take the top echelon, starting with Carol, who has the roundest heels in America." Tompkins glanced at Peter. "Pardon me for my picture of your childhood sweetheart."

"Be my guest," Peter said.

"Carol, of course, is Mark Fleming's target. He'll have to he-man it with every doll on the lot just to keep his reputation intact, but Carol is his target number one. Complicating this is the presence at Marlingham of Mr. Francis X. Garrity, the soft-drink tycoon, who is momentarily Carol's husband. The top supporting actor—playing Carol's husband in the film—is Orrin Pell, who between Carol's marriages number two and three was her very special boy friend. The Atomic Energy Commission is missing something in high-explosive content."

"You've missed one step," Peter said. "How did they all come to gather at Marlingham?"

"The Monster was looking for a location to shoot his epic," Tompkins said. "It happens that one of the banks financing the picture also holds the mortgage on Marlingham. They arranged a meeting between The Monster and Clarissa Moffet. The Monster knew the minute he looked at Marlingham that it was exactly what he wanted—must have. Clarissa played it with unexpected shrewdness. She asked a fabulous price: a hundred and fifty thousand for six months, and fifty thousand for an option to renew the lease for another six months at the same figure. Even Monty Spain might have turned his back on those telephone numbers, but Clarissa played her cards too well for him.

" 'Marlingham will be in the spotlight of a public circus and scandal,' she told Monty Spain. 'I don't want that. I don't want your kind of people making a public peepshow and shambles out of my memories of a long and happy life at Marlingham. I know my price is too high, Mr. Spain, but if you should be willing to meet it, I couldn't afford to refuse.' "

Tompkins laughed and waved his empty glass at Juan. "The Monster might have walked away from any other approach, dearly as he wanted Marlingham. But to be told he wasn't desirable is something he couldn't and wouldn't take. He promptly signed the lease." Tompkins' smile faded. "Knowing him, I wonder just how he'll go about making Clarissa Moffet pay for that insult before he's through with Marlingham." He shrugged. "So there it is, old boy. Marlingham and its current charge of TNT—including the subject of your first inquiry, the unexpected Mr. Francis X. Garrity."

Peter leaned forward and knocked his pipe out in the glass ash tray on the table. "Thanks for so much very useful detail, Bill. One more question if I may."

"Shoot."

"What is Montague Spain's reputation with women?"

Tompkins laughed. "He eats 'em for breakfast," he said. "But he likes them cheap and dumb, and he likes them without fanfare. Hollywood is full of little girls who thought Monty Spain's custom-built bed was the road to stardom."

"Ever any rumors about him and Carol?"

Tompkins looked interested. "Not that I ever heard of. The Monster doesn't go for the famous glamor girls. I have a theory about it."

"Which is?"

"He doesn't want to risk having a public 'no' said to him," Tompkins said.

3

THAT NIGHT Peter Styles came very close to the decision to forget about Carol Richmond and her husbands and lovers—present, past, and future. Carol, and Spain, and Mark Fleming and the rest lived in a world that played by its own rules, dramatizing as a matter of business the kind of emotional conflicts that are normally kept private in other segments of our society. The more gossip and chat about Marlingham and its colorful tenants, the bigger the build-up for Monty Spain's forthcoming picture. For Peter to become involved, to lend his particular prestige as a reporter and commentator to the scene, would simply enhance Monty Spain's future box office returns. Carol's dramatic statements about someone trying to destroy her as an actress and person and that her husband might be "her enemy" were probably just a sample of the "larger-than-life" techniques of the theater and Hollywood.

Having decided to forget it, Peter couldn't sleep. There must be hundreds of people with whom Carol had been close in the last twenty years—both male and female. She must have some women friends! Why turn for help, if she really needed help, to someone she hadn't seen since she was fourteen years old? Was it just an act to build up the high-powered promotion for the picture? Peter tried to make himself think so, but finally he stopped because it just wouldn't make sense that way. His own personal radar system had detected real fear in Carol.

Six or seven months before that night, Peter had returned to Darlbrook Lodge in Vermont, the scene of his accident, in the hope of getting on the trail of the "joy-killers" who had murdered his father and cost him a section of his right leg. He never got on their trail, but he found himself projected into the center of the particularly brutal murder of two girls, at Darlbrook for a week end of skiing. He was not a detective, but he'd been instrumental in solving the case and gotten a good deal of unwanted publicity for his accomplishment. Carol would almost certainly have read about it at the time. Had she then decided that her childhood friend had special gifts for helping her with her problem, whatever it was? Lying in his bed, staring up at the darkness, Peter decided that Carol's cry for help had been genuine. The least he could do was to make an opportunity for her to tell him what she had not been able to tell him in the presence of her husband, the soft-drink tycoon.

Having made up his mind to that, Peter slept.

The next morning Peter laid the groundwork for a visit to Marlingham. He got *Newsview*'s editor, Frank Devery, to call Monty Spain's public relations man with the news that he wanted his top writer to do a feature story on the making of a Spain epic. They bit at the suggestion like a hungry fish. A feature in *Newsview* would reach millions of readers, and a feature by Peter Styles would have a quality and prestige that the gossip columnists couldn't provide. Peter must come, by all means! Peter must allow them to put him up at Marlingham, where he could see everything at close range! Anything Peter wanted, they would provide!

It was early afternoon when Peter left New York in his white Jaguar convertible, heading up the East River Drive, with a bag packed for a two or three days' stay at Marlingham. Once there, even if Carol's call for help was a melodramatic fake, he might find material for a piece of some kind.

After two and a half hours of driving through the bright fall colors, deepening as he headed north, he came, after stopping to inquire in the village of Chadwick, to the stone gates that marked the entrance to Marlingham. High up on a hill, almost a mile away, he saw the great house. He had to stop at the gate, however, because there was a heavy chain stretched between the two stone pillars. A man came out of a little stone gatehouse and approached him.

"What do you want here?" the man asked sullenly.

"I think I'm expected. I'm Peter Styles."

Instantly the man was all smiles and courtesy. "You bet, Mr. Styles. Mr. Samuels is waiting for you up at the house."

Ron Samuels was the name of the public relations man.

"We have to keep this chain up," the man said, "Because there's so damn many sightseers and Peeping Toms around. Open right up for you."

The winding bluestone drive started out through woods, skirted the private golf course, cut along what Peter guessed was the famous trial course for jumping horses. He could see the brush jumps, fence and rails, and stone wall obstacles with their white wooden wings. He was just reaching the edge of acres of beautiful lawn, planted with shrubs, evergreens and silver birch trees, when something caught his eye.

It was a riderless horse, charging up across the lawn, reins and stirrups flapping. It was a black horse, spirited, head held high. He stopped, maybe fifty yards away, staring at the slowly approaching white car. Then he lowered his head, whirled around, and raced away over a rise of ground, tearing great divots in the lawn, and disappeared over a rise of ground.

The animal had a curious impact on Peter. He remembered the day that he had stood in a window, high above a Washington street, watching the funeral cortege of President Kennedy. Ninety per cent of all the people in America were watching it, either in person or on television. Grief, shock, and anger—and in some rare cases, Peter guessed, a ghoulish pleasure—were the order of the day. For each watcher there must have been something special, some detail that stood out above everything else. For some it must have been the gallantry and courage of the widow; for others the parade of great world figures walking humbly on foot; for others the dramatic church service; for others the grief-stricken faces at the grave side, caught unguarded by vigilant cameras.

All of those things had impressed Peter, but the one thing he hadn't been able to erase from his memory afterwards was the riderless black horse being led behind the caisson, never still, always the picture of enormous, restless energy, difficultly controlled. Peter had the feeling that the spirit of the dead man was reflected in that magnificent black Dybbuk horse. When he disappeared from view, Peter waited, breathing hard, somehow afraid that he might be gone. The horse seemed to Peter to represent something unquenchable, indestructible, that the dead President had left behind him.

The riderless black horse at Marlingham, visible again now on another rise of ground, brought that all back to Peter. He realized he'd stopped his car to watch, a curious prickling sensation running along his spine.

A riderless horse, in the open like that, suggested a fallen rider. Peter turned slightly in his seat to look out over the jumping course.

The afternoon had grown unusually dark. A late fall thunderstorm was in the offing. Black clouds moved slowly toward Marlingham, and Peter saw a jagged streak of lightning split the distant blackness. And then he saw the man.

He was a good two hundred yards away from where Peter had stopped his car. He lay spreadeagled, face down, on the rich green turf directly in front of one of the stone wall jumps. There was no sign of movement.

Peter looked around for help and saw none. Then he swung his car off the road and headed toward the fallen rider, across a bumpy field. He had to stop some distance away because the terrain was too rough for the low-slung Jaguar. Running over rough ground was still something of a problem for Peter, but he managed with a kind of skipping step. Just before he reached the man, he looked back over his shoulder. Far up near the house he saw a Jeep with several people in it headed toward him.

Then he reached the man. Before he touched him, instinct told him that help was useless. The man's head was turned away to one side at a grotesque angle. Peter had seen broken necks before, during his service in Korea with the Marine Corps.

The fallen man wore tan riding breeches, black boots, and a gray tweed riding jacket. A soft black hat rested on his head, almost as if it had been dropped there after the fall.

Peter felt for a pulse in one of the outstretched wrists. There was none. Gently he put his arm under the man and turned him slowly over.

Peter's breath made a hissing sound between his teeth.

A garish clown was revealed: white clown makeup from hairline to collar, a bright red nose and drooping scarlet mouth, little black crosses on the closed eyelids. A clown, dressed in swank, tailored riding clothes.

Peter leaned closer, eyes narrowed. The man had apparently been thrown when the black horse refused the stone wall jump. Deep slashes in the moist green turf showed where the horse had set his feet and slid for a few yards in refusing. Only by looking closely could Peter see the abrasion on the dead man's left temple where his head had struck the wall. It wasn't instantly noticeable because there'd been very little bleeding. More particularly it wasn't noticeable because the clown makeup had been put on over the wound. After the fall. *After he was dead!*

Peter lowered the body to the grass and stood up. Voices were behind him. People were running toward him from the Jeep which had stopped only a few yards away.

Someone grabbed his arm and pulled him around. It was a small, gnomish man, eyes hidden by black glasses, with an angry slit of a mouth.

"Who the hell are you and what are you doing here?" the gnome demanded.

Peter noticed two other men, both kneeling by the body, both wearing black glasses. "My name is Peter Styles," he said. "I was driving up from the front gates when I saw that riderless horse. Then I spotted him—" He gestured toward the dead clown.

"Mr. Styles!" The gnome was all smiles, "I'm Ron Samuels. I've been expecting you." His handshake was unexpectedly firm.

"Whoever he is, he's dead," Peter said, still looking at the clown.

The two kneeling men were staring at each other. One of them, wearing a beret, looked at Samuels and Peter.

"What kind of a gag is this?" he asked, obviously not expecting an answer.

"Louis, this is Peter Styles," Samuels said. "Louis Beaujon, our assistant director."

Beaujon nodded without rising. "You found him like this, Mr. Styles?"

"He was lying face down. I turned him over."

"This absurdity? This makeup?"

"Just as I found him."

Beaujon muttered something under his breath in French. The second man stood up. Nobody bothered to introduce him to Peter.

"Who is he?" Peter asked.

"Rex Barton, a bit actor in the picture," Samuels said. "Fortunately expendable."

Peter's head turned sharply. "Expendable?"

Samuel's mouth twitched, as though he was trying not to laugh at a private joke in public. "That sounded a little cold-blooded, didn't it? In an operation like this you get to think only of the production. Barton can be replaced with very little money cost at this stage of the game. It could have been someone else who's already on thousands of feet of film."

"What is the significance of the clown face?"

Samuels shrugged. "Some kind of joke. We're lousy with jokes around here, Mr. Styles."

"A bad one," Peter said. "The makeup was put on his face after he was dead."

"You're kidding!"

"Look for yourself."

Samuels and Beaujon exchanged quick looks from behind their black glasses. The other man stood to one side. He was smiling, of all things.

"We'd better carry him up to the house," Beaujon said.

"You'd better leave him exactly where he is," Peter said. "Even an accidental death is a matter for the police."

"The police!" Beaujon said. Behind the black lenses

Peter thought he could almost hear the assistant director wondering what this would mean to "the production."

Samuels shrugged and laughed. The dead man might have been a grotesque stage prop. "A story's a story, Louis. All grist to the mill as long as they spell our names right." Beaujon turned to the silent smiler. "Marshall, you'd better go up to the house and call the State Police."

"Okay, Louis." He started for the Jeep.

"I'll take you up to the house, Styles," Samuels said. He glanced up at the sky. "It's going to rain hard in a few minutes."

"I'll stay here," Peter said. "The troopers will want to talk to me, since I found him."

Something had clicked in the back of Peter's mind when the third man had been addressed as "Marshall." Then it fell into place. "Marshall is waiting outside in the car for us," Francis X. Garrity had told Carol the night before.

Rain started to fall in big warning drops. Louis Beaujon took off his tweed jacket and spread it gently over the dead man's face. "Can we take cover in your car, Mr. Styles?" he asked.

They went to the Jaguar and sat huddled together on the two bucket seats. The rain suddenly came down in sheets, almost hiding the dead body from them.

"One of you got a cigarette?" Beaujon asked. "I left mine in my jacket pocket."

Samuels extracted a cigarette from the breast pocket of his sports shirt. Peter held the car lighter for him. Beaujon took off his black glasses and wiped the rain spots from them with a handkerchief. With the glasses off, he became something more than a face painted on a flat wall. He had been a very handsome man once upon a time. He looked tired and defeated now; the lines at the corners of a good mouth were deeply chiseled; a network of lines at the corners of sad brown eyes made him look as if he were wincing slightly from some chronic pain.

"Poor devil," he said.

"When you gotta go, you gotta go," Samuels said.

"Shut up," Beaujon said. Then after a pause: "He used to be a pretty good actor. He came to me for a job in this opera. He'd worked for me, worlds ago, in France. He needed the job badly. He's got a wife somewhere and a kid with muscular distrophy. Monty let me cast the bit parts, so I hired him. I shouldn't have. All the small parts in this thing have to be able to ride. Hunting scenes. Rex hadn't been on a horse since he was a kid. He told me that, frankly, but he was sure if he had a few days to freshen up—" Beaujon shrugged. "The hunting scenes are coming up two or three days from now. He was trying to squeeze in practice every spare moment he had. He knew if he looked bad on the first dry run, Monty would fire him without any second chance."

"I never knew you were a sentimentalist, Louis," Samuels said.

"I always knew you were a first-class louse," Beaujon said sharply. He put his black glasses back on, hiding once more any revelation of his personal emotions.

Samuels seemed unperturbed. He looked at Peter. "After all the years he's been in it, Louis still hasn't learned that you have to laugh at everything that happens or cut your throat."

"I'm supposed to be a connoisseur of perverted senses of humor," Peter said. "What's the clown joke?"

Two pairs of black glasses turned on him.

"Clown joke?" Beaujon asked.

"Is there a clown in the script?"

"No."

"Is a clown face some sort of private joke on the lot?"
"Not that I've heard of—and I hear," Samuels said.
"No joke about clowns," Beaujon said. The end of his cigarette glowed red. "It's grotesque. You saw no one anywhere near him when you came out here, Mr. Styles?"
"No one. Whoever painted his face had gone."
Beaujon lowered the car window a couple of inches to toss out his cigarette. Wind and rain buffeted the Jaguar. "I saw Rex just when he was starting out. That was more than an hour before you found him. The horse could have been running loose down here long before we saw him up on the lawns. Plenty of time for the joker to do his job and go away."
"Was Barton involved in any special feuds or jealousies on the lot?" Peter asked.
Beaujon shook his head. "Quiet fellow, Mr. Styles. Worried about his lines; worried about his riding problem; worried about his kid. He stayed very much to himself."
"Oh, we've got feuds for you, Mr. Styles," Samuels said. "But I don't think Rex was involved in any of them."
"Someone evidently wanted to make fun of his dying," Peter said.
The storm swept by and in the west the late afternoon sun suddenly shone brightly in their eyes. Beaujon got out of the car and walked over to the sodden figure on the ground.
"Louis's one of the few nice people on this job," Samuels said. His bantering tone was gone for the moment. He looked at Beaujon, squatting beside the dead man, doing nothing. Just keeping the late Rex Barton company.
"Assistant director?"
Samuels nodded. "He was one of the bright young boys in France before the war," Samuels said. "Fought in the French army and then in the Resistance. Never seemed to

be able to get in the groove after that. Lost something, I guess. He told me once that, after what he'd been through, making movies somehow didn't seem very important. But like you and me, he has to eat. Monty picked him up some ten years ago when he was making a picture on the Riviera. He's been part of Monty's staff ever since. His title is Assistant Director, but nobody assists Monty with the actual directing. He takes care of everything, down to the smallest scenes, himself. Louis is a sort of trouble shooter; takes care of fractured nerves and damaged egos. He's the one you go to when you can't stand it any more but have to!" Samuels' laugh was mirthless.

Not far away they heard the low growl of a siren. The troopers were coming.

There wasn't much to the police inquiry at that time. A Sergeant Tresh was in charge, with a trooper named Childers to assist him. Even after the rain the markings in the turf were pretty clear. Barton had obviously been thrown against the stone wall jump when the horse refused. Only the clown face was bothersome, and the two young troopers didn't seem to take it too seriously.

"You didn't see anyone around, Mr. Styles?" Tresh asked.

"No."

"You didn't know Barton?"

"No. I don't know what he looks like now."

"Crazy gag," Childers said.

Tresh looked at Samuels. They'd evidently had dealings before. "It would be nice to have an explanation of it, Ron," he said. "Not much doubt the death was accidental. But that face! I mean it's got to go in our report, and the Lieutenant is likely to ask me questions."

"I'll nose around," Samuels said. "If you're through with Mr. Styles, there are a lot of people anxiously waiting for him up at the house."

"Guess you can't add anything to what you've told us, can you, Mr. Styles?"

"Not now," Peter said.

Two troopers and two pairs of black glasses looked at him, questioning.

"As a reporter, I'm as interested in the answers as you are, Sergeant," Peter said.

Marlingham's entrance hall was big enough to accommodate a good-sized ball. There was a field stone fireplace facing you as you came in, and hanging over the mantel was a huge copper shield with the Marlingham coat of arms in red, white and green enamel, done in some sort of inlay work. Two great high-backed chairs made of a dark wood that might have been teak, elaborately carved, stood on either side of the hearth. A mammoth oriental rug covered the parquet floor, some sort of Byzantine battle scene spread out before you. In the center of the hall was a long stretcher table, made of the same wood as the chairs and with the same elaborate carving by some long-forgotten Eastern craftsman. Copper trays for calling cards rested on it. On the walls were a collection of priceless Japanese prints. Like so many old-time New Englanders, an early Moffet had collected art objects brought in by the trading ships. You weren't supposed to make yourself comfortable in this hall. You were just to wait here to be summoned.

When Peter had driven up under the porte-cochere in the Jaguar, accompanied by Samuels, the man named Marshall, now wearing a white houseman's coat—but still hidden behind the black glasses—was there to take Peter's bag.

"Marshall will take your things up to your room and take care of the car," Samuels said. "But before you settle in, I'd like to take you to meet Monty. He's expecting us."

You didn't keep Monty Spain waiting, it appeared.

They walked down a mirror-lined corridor to a door at the end of it. Samuels knocked. A deep voice growled a command to "come in."

The room beyond the door was a study, lined with books, an old-fashioned, very beautiful roll-top desk in one corner. In the center of the room two men sat at a card table playing a game. The one facing the door was the only person in the world who could be Montague Spain. Bill Tompkins had been right, Peter thought. Peter found he really wasn't prepared for this bearded mountain of a man. He was scowling at the cards held in one hamlike hand—a carefully manicured hand. He was wearing gray flannel slacks, a white shirt open at a massive, corded throat, a silk scarf tied Ascot fashion and tucked into the shirt, and a blue blazer with brass buttons, and the emblem of some long-forgotten yacht club sewed to the breast pocket.

The Monster didn't look up from his cards at they came in. The heavily hooded eyes concentrated on his hand.

"Your draw, Francis," he said, without looking up.

The man with his back to Peter was the soft-drink tycoon who was married to Carol Richmond. His slender hand reached out and picked up a card from the center pile. The pause had all the implications of life and death.

"I hear Rex Barton got himself killed," The Monster said without looking up.

"Yes, sir," Samuels said.

Francis X. Garrity discarded. The Monster's bearded mouth moved in a sinister smile as he reached for the discard.

"Accidental?"

"Yes, sir."

The hooded eyes lifted to look at Francis X. Garrity. "Gin!" The Monster said. "Surely you knew I was saving sevens, Francis."

"I had it figured another way," Garrity said. "Forty-two points here." He tossed down his hand.

The Monster wrote something on a slip of paper and at last he looked up at his visitors.

"Who's this?" he asked.

"Peter Styles, sir," Samuels said.

Peter turned and started for the door.

"Wait!" The Monster bellowed.

Peter turned. "If you can choose your time for recognizing me, Spain, I guess I can choose my time for recognizing you. See you around."

And he went out, closing the door softly behind him.

4

PETER WALKED down the corridor toward the entrance hall, slightly annoyed with himself for having indulged in the childish pleasure of telling off The Monster. He understood a little better what Bill Tompkins had been talking about now. It was part of Spain's technique to get you off base before you had a chance to maneuver. The Monster had started a war with the new arrival before they'd had a chance to exchange hellos.

Samuels came galloping along the corridor behind Peter. "Wrong approach," he said, falling into step beside Peter.

"I'm here to write a story," Peter said, "not to be kicked around by that fat egomaniac."

"You can catch more flies with honey et cetera," Samuels said.

"I'm not here to catch flies—or am I?" Peter said.

"He's a passionate gin rummy player," Samuels said. "Not even God can interrupt him in the middle of a hand. Garrity is his prime sucker at the moment. He must have lost seven or eight thousand bucks to the boss in the month we've been here."

"I gather he can afford it," Peter said.

"Just trying to put you on the right track," Samuels said. He stopped at the foot of a graceful winding stair that led to the second floor, glancing at his wrist watch. "Your room is the second to the left at the top of the stairs." he said. "Marshall will have put your stuff there. The cocktail lounge is just down this corridor on the right. Everybody'll be gathering there in about twenty minutes for the martini derby. You'll find the makings in your room if you don't want to wait, plus a bottle of your brand of bourbon."

"How do you know my brand?" Peter asked.

Samuels grinned. "My job not to make mistakes. I called your office to inquire."

The room assigned to Peter was a decorator's dream. A magnificent canopied four-poster bed that must have dated back to Revolutionary times, a Governor Winthrop desk, a polished chest of drawers that stood taller than Peter, two beautiful hooked rugs, a round duck-legged table near a high-backed arm chair covered in an old gray and pink chintz had a silver ice bucket on it, a bottle of gin, a bottle of bourbon, a bottle of vermouth, a siphon of soda, glasses and pitchers.

Four windows looked out over the immense lawns and gardens of the estate. Peter took a look in the bathroom. It was fabulous. A sunken black marble tub, a black marble washbasin, and a very modern glassed-in shower.

Marshall had not only delivered Peter's luggage, he had unpacked it, hung the extra suit, sports jacket and slacks, and dinner jacket in a huge walk-in closet. Extra shoes were neatly racked. His toilet articles had all been placed in the bathroom cabinet.

He was in residence.

He'd only just completed his inspection of his quarters when there was a soft knock at the door. It was Marshall, still white-coated and still wearing his black glasses although darkness had begun to settle over the world.

"Everything okay?" he asked.

"Fabulous," Peter said.

"Quite a joint," Marshall said. The language didn't go with a houseman in such elegant surroundings. Nor did his casual fishing of a cigarette out of his pocket and lighting it. "They say the Moffets entertained royalty here more than once."

"Straighten me out on something," Peter said. "You work for the Garritys, or Spain, or who?"

Marshall's smile was wide and white. "Francis X. is my boss," he said. "But it was Carol who arranged to have you put in this room. They don't do so well by most of the press."

Peter's curiosity mounted. The use of Carol's first name —so casual—certainly didn't fit the role of houseman.

"I been with Francis ever since I was a kid," Marshall said, evidently sensing Peter's unspoken question. "Like one of the family."

"Nice work if you can get it," Peter said.

"Make you a drink?"

"Thanks. Bourbon on the rocks."

"Martinis are the order of the day downstairs," Marshall said. "Unless you're a drink mixer, I advise—"

"Fine. Make it a martini. Dry."

"In and out?"

"How's that?"

"Francis just likes the vermouth swirled around in the glass and then poured off. In and out, we call it."

"That sounds dry."

Marshall made the drink expertly. Ice was put in the glass and stirred around until it was chilled. The drink, mixed in a glass pitcher, was only a martini by courtesy. There was only the faint aroma of vermouth, but none that Peter could see actually remaining in it. A twist of lemon sprayed its surface gently.

"Francis always dresses for dinner," Marshall said, "but he's the only one. You'll be okay the way you are."

"Thanks, Marshall. The drink is excellent."

"You might as well call me Buck. Everyone does," Marshall said. " 'Nother drink?"

"Thanks, no."

Buck Marshall hesitated. "Make anything out of that clown business yet?"

"No. Have you?"

Marshall laughed. "One thing about this layout," he said. "Nothing's unexpected. Everybody hates everybody, and they got odd ways of showing it. Only thing about that—Barton was a loner. I'd have said nobody had it in for him."

"Maybe nobody did," Peter said. "He was dead. Maybe he was just a convenient signboard for a joke of some kind."

"I hadn't thought of that," Marshall said. "Could be. Well, let me know if you need anything, Peter."

So much for the well-trained houseman.

Peter had to remind himself that the bizarre decoration of a corpse out on the jumping course was not his primary reason for being at Marlingham. He'd come here in answer to a cry for help from Carol Richmond. In any case there was no possibility of making an intelligent guess about the clown face until he had a clearer picture of the temporary world of Marlingham. That world was about to convene for its pre-dinner cocktail hour.

Peter changed out of his sports jacket and slacks into a dark blue worsted lounging suit and went downstairs to look for what Samuels had called the cocktail lounge.

He found it by ear. There was a volume of talk and

laughter down the corridor to his left. The picture people had turned a small living room into their drinking room. There was a temporary bar set up at the end of a long narrow room. Whatever the furnishings of this place had been originally, they'd been replaced by a dozen small round tables with accompanying chairs. One long overstuffed couch confronted a fireplace at one side. A spinet piano occupied another corner, and a young man was playing some current show tunes with half a dozen people grouped around him.

The first marked impression Peter had was that almost all of the twenty-five or thirty people in the room wore black glasses, despite the fact that it was evening and the room's lighting was soft.

He stood in the doorway, unnoticed for the moment. He saw Carol at the far end of the room at a table with her husband and a man he knew from photographs to be Mark Fleming. There was a dark, handsome, lush-looking young woman at the table with them. Monty Spain and his assistant Louis Beaujon were at the opposite side of the room engaged in conversation with an unidentifiable man.

Then Carol saw him.

She came across the room to him, almost running.

"Peter darling!" she said, as she reached him. "Bless you!" She reached up on tiptoe and kissed his cheek.

Before he could do more than say hello, Francis X. Garrity had joined them, a thin smile on his lips, staring blandly at Peter through his owlish glasses.

"Welcome to our city," he said.

On Garrity's heels was Mark Fleming. Instantly Peter felt this man's curious physical magnetism. His face was square and rugged. He wasn't quite as tall as Peter, but he suggested height. He moved with the kind of threatening grace you might connect with a tiger. He had the most intense and the brightest blue eyes Peter ever remembered seeing. His smile had a sort of sardonic quality, as if he knew why Peter was really here and was telling him at the very start that it was all a waste of time. Peter had the feeling he'd been evaluated and not found dangerous.

Fleming had two cocktail glasses in his hand. He handed one to Peter as Garrity introduced them. "You can't enter this world dry, Mr. Styles," he said. His voice was deep with an electric vitality to it.

Dozens of pairs of black glasses turned to the door. Peter, Fleming, Garrity, and Monty Spain, at the far end of the room, seemed to be the only people present, including the bartenders and waiters, not hiding behind the black lenses. It made everyone look masked.

"I call it the Black Glass City," Fleming said. "It keeps you from seeing what they're thinking. But I can help you out. Everyone in this room is wondering whether we're going to get a pan or a plug from the famous Peter Styles. Which is it to be?"

"How can I tell at this point?" Peter said. He lifted his cocktail glass and drank.

Carol slipped her arm through his. "Join us at our table, Peter. And if you pay too much attention to Sherry, I'll scratch her eyes out."

"Sherry?"

"Don't tell me you didn't recognize Sherry Garth." Carol indicated the dark girl who had remained at their table.

"I'm afraid she isn't even a name to me," Peter said.

"The new Ava Gardner," Carol said. Her fingers tightened on Peter's arm. "My rival in the picture—and in other ways."

They reached the table. The dark girl looked up at Peter through her opaque lenses, a kind of impudent smile on her bright red lips. "It's going to be pleasant meeting a famous man who won't have to remind us every five minutes of how good he is," she said. Her voice was low and sultry. A quick little glance at Fleming gave an edge to her words. She must have been ten years younger than Carol, which would make any rivalry between them a bitter business for the older woman.

Fleming drew up an extra chair, and they all sat at the table. Peter put his half-empty glass down. It disappeared instantly and was replaced by a full one.

"You've already created a sensation here, darling," Carol said.

"Oh?"

"You did something not another person in this room would dare to do," Carol said. She laughed delightedly. "You walked out on The Monster and left him with his mouth hanging open. Francis says he was boiling."

"He likes to impress," Garrity said. "I trust he doesn't own stock in the magazine you work for, Styles. He never forgets a brush-off."

"Mr. Styles looks as if he could take care of himself," Sherry Garth said.

Peter grinned at her. "I'm not scared," he said.

"Just what is your slant to be on The Black Glass City?" Fleming asked. "Gossip, I know, isn't your dish."

Peter hesitated. He saw Carol's mouth tighten at the corners. "We live in a strange world, Fleming," he said. "Thousands of different groups of people, isolated from each other in aims, in ethics, in culture, in degrees of freedom. I suppose what I'm always looking for as an observer is some common bond that holds us together in one whole structure. If it isn't there, the whole thing is going to come tumbling down around our ears. I'm interested in your special little world here. What lies behind its flamboyance, its fake front? What links you to a common purpose that gives us all a reason for living?"

"And that purpose is—?" Fleming asked.

"I haven't found the answer to that," Peter said. "But if it's no more than individual survival, we're all going to come unstuck in a hurry."

"A prophet of doom," Garrity said, holding his drink up to the light.

A little shudder seemed to run over Sherry Garth's beautiful shoulders. "Prophets make me uneasy," she said. "It's hard enough to live day by day, without having someone tell you in advance what will happen tomorrow." A light from somewhere reflected in her black glasses, making two little dancing orange dots. "But if you are a prophet, Peter Styles, perhaps you can tell whether or not we'll find out who thought it was so bloody funny to desecrate the body of a dead man this afternoon. I understand you found him."

Peter reached for his glass and found it had been refilled again. Martinis were dished out here like water. The ones down here, by the way, couldn't match the one Buck Marshall had made for him up in his room.

"Poor Rex." Carol sounded far away.

"You knew him in the old days, didn't you, darling?" Francis X. Garrity asked, in that smooth voice that might or might not have extra meaning to it.

"Yes," Carol said in a clipped way that suggested she'd heard that extra meaning in her husband's question.

Peter was aware that the room was intolerably hot. Had Garrity been implying something? Somehow it seemed tangled up. The piano sounded very loud. Sherry Garth was leaning forward, looking at him intently. She was, he thought, waiting for an answer to her question.

What had the question been?

It was then that Peter realized that three martinis had knocked him completely on his ear. He was conscious of little beads of sweat on his forehead.

"Hello, Dolly," the piano player sang, over his rhythmic beat.

Fleming, his bright blue eyes fixed on Peter's face, laughed. The sound reached Peter like a hollow echo from the bottom of a well. He pushed back his chair and stood up, and the whole room began to spin around him. He turned his head and it seemed to him that hundreds of round, glittering black glass eyes stared at him.

He stumbled as he turned, and someone had him firmly by the arm. Through his head passed the calm assurance that this was some kind of nightmare. He was a mature man of thirty-six years, an accustomed drinker, who no more got bowled over on three martinis than he would on three glasses of milk. But the room kept spinning.

"Walk! Hang onto me and walk, straight and easy as you can," a voice whispered in his ear.

He turned and saw the door to the hall several thousand yards away. It was a woman who had him by the arm and he glanced down at a dark head. Sherry Garth?

"Hello, Dolly!"

Later he couldn't have told you whether he walked or staggered to the door. Out in the hall he made quite sure that his good Samaritan was Sherry Garth. Her face was white, tense with anger.

"That miserable fat bastard," she said, her voice harsh. "Where's your room?"

"Second floor—second on the left," he muttered.

"Elevator, buster," she said. "Walk!"

How he managed, he couldn't say. Suddenly there was a clang of metal, a whirring sound, and a sickening rise that turned his stomach upside down.

"Hang on!"

He was stumbling now, reaching out for the wall to

steady himself. Then they walked from bright light into a blessedly cool darkness.

"Let me help you off with your coat."

"No, just—"

"Stand still!" Sherry Garth ordered.

She tugged off his coat and suddenly he was whirling downward onto a soft heaven—his bed. He made a superhuman effort to collect himself.

"What miser'ble fat bastard?" he asked thickly.

"The Monster!" Sherry said in that harsh voice. "You gave him the brush and he had them slip you a mickey. Wanted you to make a shameful fool of yourself in public. Lie still!"

Cool fingers loosened his tie and undid the collar button of his shirt. A soft eiderdown was pulled up over him.

"Tomorrow," Peter muttered.

"What?"

"Thank you tomorrow—dear Miss Garth."

"Do you want me to call a doctor?"

Peter didn't hear the question. A nauseous darkness had engulfed him.

Peter opened his eyes. A reddish-gray light was around him. The light of dawn, he realized. He was lying on his bed, in his room at Marlingham, and he felt like hell. His head was splitting and his mouth felt as if it was full of hot, dry cardboard. He turned his head to see if there was a water pitcher or thermos on his bedside table.

And he tried to remember what had happened. The martinis must have knocked him cold. Then, vaguely, he remembered being helped upstairs by Sherry Garth. He reached under the quilt and realized he was still dressed except for his suit jacket.

He had to get to the bathroom for cold water. He had to

have cold water or die. And then, as he moved, he knew instinctively that his artificial leg was missing. He had no memory of taking it off.

He sat bolt upright in bed, old fears and terrors gripping him. Then he saw it, put down beside his bed, the black shoe and sock he'd been wearing the night before still on it. He must have taken it off himself—and yet he had absolutely no memory of having done. Could Sherry Garth—? No, she wouldn't have done such a thing; been guilty of such an invasion of privacy. He must have done it himself.

He swung his feet over the edge of the bed and bent down to fasten the foot and its harness to his leg. He thought the top of his head was going to fly off.

Once the leg was secure, he stood up and walked, unsteadily, to the bathroom. He turned the cold water faucet on full at the black marble basin. He leaned heavily on the basin with both his hands, wondering if at last he was going to be sick. Then, slowly, he raised his head to look at himself in the mirror.

His heart jammed hard against his ribs.

A clown looked back at him out of the glass—a white-faced clown with red button nose, a gaping red mouth turned down at the corners, and little black crosses on heavy eyelids.

Nightmare!

Peter raised his hand to touch his face, and his hand appeared in the mirror.

Sometime in the unconscious depths of the night, someone had done this to him.

Part Two

1

THE EYES of the clown face stared back at Peter from the mirror. Black lines drawn at the corners of the eyes made it look as if the clown, blinking unbelievingly, was about to cry.

A deep shuddering noise came from deep in Peter's throat. He was shaking from head to foot. Shock and anger; growing, blazing, gut-tearing anger.

The next part of the joke, he thought, would be for someone to "discover" him this way. He moved quickly out of the bathroom to the door of his bedroom. He shot home the black, wrought-iron slide bolt and leaned against the door trying to control his teeth-chattering shakes.

He glanced at the bed. There was a gooseneck lamp on the bedside table, and the flexible neck had been turned in such a way so that the last time the lamp was lit it must have shone directly on the pillow—directly on Peter's face as he lay there in a deep, drugged sleep.

Because there was no doubt of it in his mind now. He hadn't suddenly developed a vulnerability to martinis. Out of the fog of last night came the memory of Sherry Garth's angry voice. "*You gave him the brush and he had them slip you a mickey!*" No question of it, he had been drugged, and then, alone and helpless, someone had come into his room, had deliberately unfastened his leg harness and removed his artificial leg and foot, and then painted this obscene clown makeup on his face—a face identical in every detail with one painted on the dead Rex Barton yesterday.

"Sonofabitch!" Peter whispered between his clenched teeth.

He walked back to the bathroom, his head still splitting with pain. The first thing to do was get this comic mask off his face. He felt as if it was something unclean, festering.

Hot water and soap did almost nothing to it. He felt a rising panic. If he had to call for help, the whole miserable business would become public. Actors, he knew, used cold cream to remove makeup. There was no cold cream in his kit. Then he made an almost hysterical little sound of relief. In the cabinet was a jar of special ointment he used on the stump of his leg when it sometimes became irritated from its contact with the artificial foot. His hands shook as he unscrewed the lid from the blue jar. He put a great gob of the ointment on his face and rubbed.

His breath whistled out between his teeth. A handful of Kleenex he pulled out of the container on the wall came away white, with smears of red and black. The ointment would do the job.

It took him a good ten minutes to remove every last speck of the ghoulish mask. He leaned on the black marble basin staring at his normal face in the mirror. He was sweating as though he'd had a workout in a gym. He felt physically exhausted—and relieved. At least no one would see the grotesquerie. No one but the person who had invaded his room, dared to expose his mutilation, and painted his face. Person or persons?

There was a tentative knock on the bedroom door.

Peter stepped out of the bathroom. "Who is it?" he called out when the knocker tried unsuccessfully to open the door.

"Buck Marshall. You okay?"

"Yes."

Marshall chuckled. "I warned you about those martinis."

"So you did."

"What about breakfast? A Bloody Mary might be a good way to start the day."

Peter shuddered. "No, thanks."

"Shall I bring your breakfast up here, or will you come down?"

"I'll come down," Peter said.

He felt an almost childish relief as he heard the footsteps retreating down the corridor. He had a sudden impulse to pack hastily, find his car, and get the hell away from Marlingham as fast as the Jag would take him. Downstairs—in the Black Glass City—eyes would stare at him, most of them just thinking that he was a man who couldn't handle his liquor. But one of them—or a group of them—would be laughing at him, imagining his shock at the moment he looked at himself in the mirror. That one—or that group—had stared curiously at the stump of his leg. God damn them!

Why? he wondered. Why the business with the leg? And even as he asked himself the question, he came up with the answer. If, unexpectedly, he'd come to while they were painting his face, there'd have been a quick switch-off of the light and escape. With his leg in place he could have sprung up out of bed, followed them, caught them.

Bastards.

Slowly Peter walked back toward the bathroom. Outside the door he took off his clothes, then sat on the edge of a chair and removed his artificial leg. He hopped into the glass-walled shower and turned on the water, taking it steaming hot, holding his raw-feeling face up into the fine spray.

His muscles ached. His head ached. The steaming hot water began gradually to relax his tensions. After a while he turned off the shower and came out of it. He rubbed himself down thoroughly with a thick towel until his skin was pink. He cleared off a space of the fogged mirror and looked at himself. He looked tired, but he looked himself.

He got his shaving things out of the cabinet and shaved carefully. His hand was still unsteady, but he managed to get through it without nicking himself. There was a tin of aspirin in his kit, and he took two with a long glass of cold water.

He hopped out into the other room, fastened his leg back on, and dressed: gray slacks, tweed jacket, a white shirt with a black-and-red-figured Players Club tie.

He went back to take a last look at the bathroom. He'd flushed the Kleenexes he'd used to clean the makeup off his face. So far as he could see, there was no trace of the strange procedure in which he'd been involved.

He didn't pack. Standing under the shower, he'd known he was not going to leave. No matter what the embarrassment or the jokes about his "passing out," he was going to stay. He was going to find the person or persons who had giggled over him in his helpless state last night, who had touched his leg, who had violated him, and he was going to make them grovel for mercy. Whatever Carol's problem was, real or faked, he was staying at Marlingham until he came face to face with the man, or woman, or people, whom he hated more than he had ever hated anyone in his life.

Peter glanced at his watch as he walked down the stairway to the main floor. It was a little after nine—fourteen hours since he'd staggered out of the cocktail lounge, supported by Sherry Garth.

The house seemed to be deserted, until Buck Marshall, in his white houseman's jacket and his black glasses, stepped out of one of the side rooms.

"There you are!" Buck said. "In here for grub."

Peter's mind was beginning to work in a more controlled fashion. The drug that had knocked him out the night before had been in a drink. There was no other way he could have taken it on. Buck Marshall had made him a drink, but he'd watched the whole process. It didn't seem possible it could have been that one. His first drink downstairs had been handed him by Mark Fleming. After that he'd been served at the table without really noticing who did it. He'd had the impression that an ubiquitous waiter had seen to it his glass was kept full.

"I heard you keeled over," Buck said. "I'd have come up to help you, but the Garth gal said you were okay."

"Slept it off," Peter said casually.

Black glasses stared at him curiously, and the man's mouth smiled. Did he know?

"Breakfast in here," Buck said.

The spacious dining room was deserted. On a sideboard, English-fashion, were half a dozen hot chafing dishes. Food seemed impossible to Peter, but the coffee, in a large glass Silex, was appealing. He crossed over and poured himself a cup.

Marshall had followed him into the room. "Actors and crew all start to work early—around six. Takes time to get on makeup and set up the day's shots. They've all 'et.' How about some tomato juice with a little Worcestershire and Tabasco in it? Warm your gut."

"Out!" a deep voice said behind Peter.

Peter turned and found himself facing Montague Spain.

The huge man filled the doorway. However flip Buck Marshall's attitude might be toward the rest of the household, he showed the profoundest respect for The Monster. He slipped through a swinging door to the kitchen like a mouse scurrying for his hole.

Spain came slowly into the room. His huge feet were encased in espadrilles. His slacks were a faded blue denim, and his hands were sunk in the pockets of a corduroy jacket. A cigarette glowed red between his lips, perilously close to his grizzled beard and mustache. His eyes were narrowed, the heavy lids almost concealing them.

"Let's start over," he said.

"Your move," Peter said, smiling a tight smile.

"Sit down," Spain said, and sat himself at the head of the big dining room table. He put out his cigarette in an ash tray and lit a fresh one.

Peter took a chair a little way down the table from the big man. He tried his coffee and it was rewarding.

"I get caught up in little games," Spain said, never taking his eyes off Peter. "The people I have to deal with are all like precocious children. I treat them that way. So, I owe you two apologies."

"Two?"

"Number one for being rude to you on your arrival yesterday. I liked the way you reacted. I like people who stand up to me. God knows there aren't many."

"And number two?" Peter said.

"I'm not a child, Mr. Styles. I know your type of man and your capacities. I know a self-controlled man when I see one. You're not someone likely to pass out on three or four martinis. You'd know when to stop. You'd know exactly how much you could take on with safety. So it's perfectly obvious that someone slipped you a Finn. I owe you an apology for that, since it happened in an establishment where I'm presumably the host. I've already set the wheels in motion to find out who did it. When I do, someone will be booted out of here so fast he won't know what hit him."

"I accept both apologies," Peter said, still smiling, "even if the last bit about the boot is unlikely to take place."

"No?"

"It doesn't seem likely that a waiter or bartender would have it in for me for any reason," Peter said. "It wouldn't make economic sense for you to boot out one of your star performers."

There was an amused glitter in Spain's narrowed eyes. "Then let's just say that my impulses in the matter are good. I take it you have no ideas about it?"

"None."

"No one here you've crossed swords with before?"

"No."

The Monster took a deep drag on his cigarette. "You're an old friend of Carol's?"

"Yes."

"I say this without meaning to throw any kind of slur at Carol. She's at the center of most of our problems here. Extraordinary girl. She generates excitement and unrest. She's an incendiary bomb. Every man on the set from stage-hand to star gets hungry in her presence. Her availability—and God knows she's made it clear over the years that she's available—doesn't make her less cherished or sought after."

"So?" Peter asked.

Spain shrugged. "An old friend coming on the scene might be dangerous to the objectives of a new friend. Maybe you were being warned off. Maybe somebody wants you to go home."

"I'm not going home," Peter said quietly. "Not till I find out who tried to make me look absurd last night."

"And then?" Spain asked, sounding interested.

"My party," Peter said.

Spain chuckled. "Hope I have a chance to be in on it. You might turn out to be a tough customer, friend."

There was something almost eager in Spain's manner. Somewhere in the back of Peter's head were echoes—the echo of Bill Tompkins wondering what Spain would do to get even with Clarissa Moffet for calling him "undesirable"; the echo of Sherry Garth's angry voice coming at him through a fog: "*You gave him the brush and he had them slip you a mickey.*" Peter watched the fat man, feeling cool and ready. Was all this friendly chat just a way of setting him up, after one knockout, for a second? It would fit the fat man's reported pleasure in keeping his hooks in a victim until it became unendurable.

Spain pushed himself up out of his chair, "I left orders for them to let me know when you put in an appearance," he said. "Wanted to speak my piece. Got to get back to work. You're welcome anywhere, Styles; on the set, on the grounds. Ask for whatever you want. We're shooting some brief scenes on the south terrace this morning, if you care to watch. Have to take advantage of this bright sunshine."

"Thanks," Peter said, not moving from his chair.

Spain paused in the doorway. "I don't blame you for being mad as hell," he said. "Whatever you do to find some answers, know that I'm on your team."

"That ought to make me a sure winner," Peter said, his smile bland.

Spain laughed, and Peter was certain it was the laughter of a man who enjoyed a little fancy swordplay. Well, if The Monster imagined he had blarneyed his way off Peter's list of suspects, he was due for a jolt.

But the truth was, Peter knew, as he walked over to the sideboard and helped himself to a hot roll and a couple of strips of bacon, kept warm and crisp on an electric hot plate, he had no list of suspects for the violence done to him during the night.

Someone had drugged a drink. No doubt of that.

Buck Marshall, who had made him a drink in his room, was unlikely suspect number one. After that it was all guesswork. Fleming had brought him his first drink, but Fleming, Carol, Francis X. Garrity, and Sherry Garth had all had access to the drinks that had come and gone on the table. Plus the bartender, the waiters, the people they passed on the way to and from the bar to the table. That eliminated absolutely no one.

Spain might have the childish motive of wanting to get even for having been less than worshiped on their first meeting. Who else?

The bland, owlish-looking Francis X. Garrity came to mind. He might not be the unjealous husband after all. He could well have resented Carol's visit to Gramercy Park. If Carol really was in trouble and her husband was her "enemy," then Garrity could have reasons for wanting Peter humiliated. Carol's "trouble," if it existed, might be the key to the whole thing. The electrical Mark Fleming might want no interference from an outsider. Carol's former lover, Orrin Pell, whom Peter hadn't as yet identified, might have similar motives. And Sherry Garth, whom Carol had marked down as a rival? Sherry had been decent and helpful in Peter's bad time, but that could have been a blind and a way of pointing a false finger at someone else—Monty Spain.

Peter leaned back in his chair and began to fill his pipe from an oilskin pouch. He was leaving out the most garish part of it all: the clown makeup. Patterns are a part of real-life crime as well as detective-story techniques. There had been a clown face on a dead actor lying on the green turf of the jumping course. There had been a clown face on a newspaper man lying in a drugged sleep on his bed. But there was absolutely no connection between himself and the late Rex Barton. They'd had only one thing in common. One, because he was dead, and the other, because he was drugged, had both been similar victims for the joker who specialized in clown faces. Neither of them had been aware of what was happening or able to resist it.

Peter held his lighter to the bowl of his pipe. Thinking about this made it more and more confusing. Was it possible that someone with a perverted sense of humor was hovering on the fringes, painting faces on the dead and the unconscious, without having any connection with the cause of death or the cause of helpless sleep? A bizarre opportunist? A sick jokesmith?

One thing, Peter felt, was working for him. Everyone at Marlingham knew that he'd passed out the night before. But only the joker who had done it—plus perhaps an accomplice or two—knew that Peter's face had been painted. For the joke to have been completely effective Peter should have been discovered with the makeup on his face—say by Buck Marshall. The news would have spread then like wildfire. Luck had saved Peter that final exposure to the big laugh. If he'd slept three or four minutes longer, Buck Marshall would have found him. As it was, the "joke" was a secret shared by Peter and the joker or jokers. Sooner or later a knowing smile, a sly remark, might put Peter on the trail. Meanwhile—?

Meanwhile he had to face the world of Marlingham, laugh off an apparent weakness for martinis, and appear to go about his legitimate business—gathering material for a *Newsview* feature on the making of a motion picture epic.

2

THE SOUTH terrace was a mass of equipment—cameras, special lights in spite of the sunshine, microphone booms, heavy cables crisscrossing the flagstone paving.

Monty Spain sat on a slightly raised platform, a white linen hat pulled forward over his eyes. Only two actors seemed to be involved in a brief scene being rehearsed, or rather, prepared for shooting. They were Sherry Garth and a dark handsome man whom Peter guessed must be Orrin Pell. Camera crew was practicing dollying a camera in from an angle into a close-up. Chalk marks were being made on the flagstones. Louis Beaujon seemed to be in charge of most of the preparations. Spain looked as though he was asleep in his mammoth chair.

Sherry Garth was sitting in a wicker armchair in the center of what was evidently to be the acting space. A makeup man knelt in front of her, powdering her face. A man, whom Peter took to be Orrin Pell's dresser, was carefully brushing the actor's dark blue jacket. Pell was inspecting his own makeup in a hand mirror.

"This goddamned shilly-shallying is costing us money!" a voice bellowed through a loud-speaker Peter couldn't spot.

The Monster, after all, was not asleep.

Louis Beaujon moved over to the platform and conferred with Spain, who made an impatient gesture with a huge hand. Beaujon picked up a hand mike.

"Dry run for the cameras," he announced to the army surrounding him. "But absolute quiet, please. Sound will be live. We are recording for sound. Places, please."

Dressers and makeup men scurried away from the actors. There were three cameras focused on the scene. A technician, wearing earphones, sat on a little wagonette mounted with equipment. The sound engineer.

Sherry Garth leaned gracefully back in her wicker chair. She was wearing jodhpurs and a white shirt, unbuttoned rather revealingly at the throat. Orrin Pell perched on the edge of a small round table beside the chair, obviously checking some chalk marks on the terrace.

"Camera check," Beaujon said.

The crews on the three cameras signaled to him.

"Sound check."

The sound engineer waved at him.

"Ready, Miss Garth and Mr. Pell?"

Neither actor moved nor gave any sign at all. Pell leaned forward toward Sherry, smiling.

"Roll!" Beaujon said.

From where he stood, Peter could hear nothing that passed between the actors. One camera dollied in close. The other two took the scene from different angles. There was evidently a brief dialogue, and then Sherry rose abruptly from her chair and slapped Pell's face. She turned and walked quickly away.

"Cut!" Beaujon said quietly.

"Was that a love pat or did you mean it for a slap, Sherry?" Spain bellowed.

The girl turned to look at the director. She stood motionless, not replying. Without the black glasses of the night before, Peter saw that she was quite breath-takingly lovely.

"The next run is for real, Sherry," Spain said. "For God sake, hit him as though you hated him. You can take it without flinching, can't you, Orrin?"

The actor nodded without turning to look at the director.

"Try to imagine he's one of those cloak-and-suitors who used to paw you over when you were a model in the garment district, Sherry," Spain said.

Someone giggled. The girl stood motionless, apparently not reacting.

A voice whispered stagily in Peter's ear: "Francis won't let me out of his sight, but I've got to talk to you, Peter. I've got to!"

He turned in time to see Carol hurrying over toward the set, a dressing robe over her clothes, followed by a maid. Almost instantly Francis X. Garrity, wearing an expertly tailored Harris tweed suit, was at Peter's elbow.

"Feeling better?" he asked genially.

"I feel fine. Slightly confused by all this," Peter said, nodding toward the set.

"I envy the recuperative powers of youth," Garrity said. "You looked in pretty bad shape last night."

"I apologize," Peter said. "Drinks hit me like a ton of bricks."

The owlish glasses looked up at Peter's face. "Monty thinks someone slipped you a Mickey Finn. Did he tell you?"

"Yes."

"Do you think so?"

"Why should anyone?" Peter asked.

"I hoped you have an answer for that. The idea intrigues me."

"Oh?"

"You'd hardly had time to make any enemies. Or had you?"

"Maybe it was somebody's unbalanced idea of a joke," Peter said. "Celebrated man-about-town passes out on three martinis."

"You take it well," Garrity said.

"Point out the guy who did it and I'll show you how well I take it," Peter said, smiling.

"Sherry Garth thinks it was Monty himslf," Garrity said. "She made quite an impassioned speech on your behalf after she'd gotten you to your room. It will undoubtedly have come to Monty's attention. That line about the garment center is the beginning of a hard time for Sherry, I'm afraid."

"You think it could have been Spain?" Peter asked.

Garrity shrugged. "You and I are outsiders in a world that's run very differently from anything we're accustomed to. People scratch and claw and yell and scream at each other in what Mark calls the Black Glass City. They hide behind glass, Styles, but they act on their emotions without leash or discipline. I smiled when you walked out on Monty in the office yesterday afternoon. He saw it. He might not forgive you for making it happen." Garrity rubbed his chin with the tips of his fingers. "Come to think of it, he may not forgive me either—for showing I was amused."

"It sounds a little farfetched," Peter said.

Garrity's laugh was dry. "Does it? Talk to me again in twenty-four hours. Hell will have broken loose somewhere before that. Are you a working reporter today, or would you like me to show you the golf course and the stables, as I promised?"

"I think I'll stay and watch," Peter said.

Garrity shrugged. "It's begun to bore me after a month. But of course it's Carol's life. Let me know when *you* get bored and we'll think up something to do together."

Garrity sauntered away in the direction of Carol who, surrounded by a little group of maid, makeup man, script girl, and a cameraman taking readings on a light meter, was evidently preparing for a scene to be worked on after the face-slapping bit. Peter watched Garrity go over to Carol, bend down and apparently speak to his wife with courteous concern, and then appropriate a nearby chair. Peter wondered about him. If he'd accepted Garrity's offer to act as tour guide of the grounds, would it have come off? If so, it would seem to mean that Peter was the object of Garrity's close watch on Carol. Did he imagine that he could keep Carol away from Peter indefinitely?

Beaujon's voice over the speaker system indicated the scene between Sherry Garth and Pell was about to be tried again.

"Places, please! This is it."

The actors took their places once more, and the camera crews signaled their readiness.

"This is a two-bit moment," Spain's voice thundered over the loud-speaker. "Let's not waste all day on it. Ready when you are."

A hand rested on Peter's sleeve and he turned to find a grinning Ron Samuels at his elbow.

"I see you lived," Samuels said.

"I'm going to have a sign printed so I don't have to keep answering that question," Peter said.

"Don't take it so hard," Samuels said. "You're not the first one to take a martini dive in these hallowed halls. Nothing very interesting going on here this morning. Couple of bits that fit in the middle of the picture somewhere. Monty's trying to make use of the morning sun on this side of the house. It doesn't last too long. There's a lady who'd like to meet you."

Samuels nodded his head toward a little rise of ground at the far end of the terrace. A tall, almost regal-looking woman stood there, a wide-brimmed straw hat covering her hair and hiding her face. She wore a tweed skirt, a chamois jacket over a white shirtwaist, and sensible-looking brown walking shoes. She wore garden gloves, and there was a basket of bright-colored fall flowers hung over her arm—mums and asters.

"The lady of the manor," Samuels said. "Mrs. Clarissa Moffet. She wants to make her pitch to you."

"Pitch?"

"She knows you're here to write a piece. She took occasion to sweet-talk your friend Bill Tompkins when he was here. Her concern is Marlingham. Bill's was Carol Richmond–Mark Fleming and company. She wants to be sure Marlingham retains its old-world dignity in the public eye, even though it's in the hands of the Philistines."

Bill Tompkins had liked Clarissa Moffet, Peter remembered. He'd called her a doll—"old-world elegance spiced with a delightful modern sense of humor."

"I supposed Mrs. Moffet was out of the picture since she'd rented the place to Spain," Peter said.

"She is and she isn't," Samuels said. "Living in the golf pro's house down by the course. One of the conditions of the lease was that she should stay somewhere on the place to supervise the care of the grounds."

"I'll be glad to talk to her," Peter said, "but don't go away. I've got a couple of questions."

Samuels' black glasses turned Peter's way, and he was smiling with a kind of impudence. "I am instructed to be your slave, Master," he said. "All you have to do is rub your lamp."

Peter glanced down at the terrace. The face-slapping scene was about to be played for the live cameras. Off to the left Carol sat in one of the garden chairs, surrounded by her entourage.

"What particular kind of trouble is Carol in at the moment?" he asked.

"Trouble?" Samuels laughed. "Perhaps we need a short course in semantics before we start the question and answer period."

"I'm willing," Peter said.

"Let's begin with the word 'trouble,' " Samuels said. He was enjoying himself. "She's only getting seven hundred and fifty thousand bucks to make this picture. She wanted more. In her book that is 'trouble.' There's a good chance that Sherry Garth will steal the female acting honors in this opera. In Carol's book that is 'trouble.' Her husband has insisted on being present twenty-four hours a day while the picture is being made. That's 'trouble.' But she plans to tumble into Mark Fleming's bed before too long, husband or no husband, former lovers or not. This will be followed by a huge explosion of some sort, followed by a noisy and sensational divorce. You and I might call this 'trouble.' Not Carol. That kind of thing is her meat and potatoes. For the first time in his life Monty Spain has his eye on a dame who rates above the chippy level. You and I might take it for granted that a girl's in trouble when Monty Spain has his eye on her. Not Carol. She's playing Monty off against Mark. Neither one of them is likely to take 'no' peaceably. Of course she may decide to play both sides of the street, which you and I would call big 'trouble.' Not Carol. So you see, when you ask me what kind of 'trouble' she's in, I have to know what you're talking about before I can answer. Our kind of 'trouble' or her kind of 'trouble'?"

"Francis Garrity will take all of this resignedly?" Peter asked.

"Ah, interesting question," Samuels said. "How did he

get Carol in the first place? She didn't need his money, God knows. He's not a stud horse like Fleming, or Orrin Pell, or some of the others who have been part of the past. He has nice manners and he makes sure she wears her rubbers when she goes out in the rain. But what else does he offer to a sex-crazy, intrigue-happy doll like Carol? What hidden charms? Or does he have some kind of secret arm lock on her? How Francis will take the explosion when it comes is one of the most interesting speculations of the day. Is the mouse really a mouse, or will he turn man-eating tiger?" Samuels laughed. "Some of us keep a weekly pool on when it will happen. The explosion, I mean. Half a dozen of the camera boys and I. This week I have Thursday. Four weeks of pool have accumulated now. If someone wins it this week, it should amount to about a hundred and seventy-five bucks."

"Where does Orrin Pell fit into this?" Peter asked.

"Alas, poor Orrin!" Samuels said. "He has no interest in Carol—except that he hates her for having publicly dropped him some years ago. He is but strictly on the trail of Miss Sherry Garth at the moment. Now that's what Carol calls 'trouble.' She doesn't want Pell for herself, but she doesn't want him publicly happy and entangled with Sherry, her rival as an actress and a woman. You can bank on it she'll try to put a spoke in that wheel. That could be a secondary explosion of some importance."

"Just one big happy family," Peter said.

"Most fun I've had since I was fourteen and caught my father in the back room of his drugstore with the lady who demonstrated cosmetics."

"You're a payload of startling information," Peter said dryly

"You asked, Master," Samuels said.

Peter felt a little shudder of distaste run along his spine.

Samuels, his real feelings concealed by the black glasses, his thin lips set in that mocking smile that suggested he was constantly on the verge of laughing at a dirty joke, was not an attractive character.

"Any new thoughts on yesterday's tragedy?" Peter asked.

"Tragedy?"

"A man died," Peter said, his voice sharp. "I haven't heard anyone mention it since it happened."

"Oh, Rex. No particular reason for anyone to dwell on it, Peter. He didn't have any close friends here. His body was shipped back to New York last night."

"Any new guesses about the clown face?" Peter asked, watching closely for any special reaction from Samuels.

There was none. "It'll come out sooner or later," he said. "Sooner or later a joker like that has to have his joke appreciated. He'll let it slip and then we'll all know." Samuels tossed away his cigarette. "Well, I got the daily releases to get out. Want me to introduce you to Mrs. Moffet, or will you handle it yourself?"

"I'll manage," Peter said.

Samuels headed for the house. Peter watched him, wondering. Nothing in this crude little man's manner had suggested he had any inkling of what had happened to Peter during the night. He was a walking gossip factory. The gossip specialists for the tabloids and the film magazines must have been delighted with that constantly running faucet of scandalous tidbits.

Down on the terrace something was still holding up the face-slapping bit. The endless time taken to get a few feet of film in the can explained in part the astronomical costs of modern film making.

3

PETER GLANCED up to the little knoll at the far end of the terrace. Clarissa Moffet was still there, looking directly at him. When their glances met, she gave him a pleasant smile. Peter crossed over and climbed the little bank of grass to her side.

"Mrs. Moffet?"

"It's a pleasure to meet you, Mr. Styles," she said in a clear cultivated voice. She held out a gloved hand to him. "I'm a fan."

"Fan?"

"Of yours, Mr. Styles." Her handshake was firm. "I read everything of yours that appears, with interest and silent applause."

Close to her he could see, under the broad brim of the straw garden hat, that this was still a very beautiful woman. The bone structure of her face suggested aristocracy in the true meaning of the word. The mouth was broad and generous, the gray eyes candid. There was a quiet dignity without a touch of stuffiness.

"I'm flattered," Peter said. "Bill Tompkins reported to me that you are a 'doll.' "

"Bill is a very nice young man, if a little shallow in his approach."

"To what?"

"All this," she said, gesturing toward the terrace. "Would you care to sit down over there on that garden bench, Mr. Styles? I do have something I'd like to talk to you about."

"I'd like that," Peter said.

She led the way to a beautifully carved marble bench set in front of a clump of lilac bushes. It was placed at an angle so that you'd have to turn your head sharply to watch what was taking place on the terrace. Clarissa Moffet put her basket of flowers down on the grass and began to pull off her garden gloves. Her hands were slender and graceful. A plain gold wedding band was the only ring she wore.

"Ten o'clock in the morning may not be the choicest time to discuss one's philosophy of life," she said. There was an amused twinkle in the gray eyes. "Do you have a cigarette?"

Peter offered his silver case and snapped on its lighter mechanism for her. "Any kind of real conversation is a lost art. I take it when and where I can find it," he said.

"Let's face it, Mr. Styles, I want something from you. There's only one reason why you might humor me and that is that you might feel a little as I do about the matter in hand."

"I may find it very hard to refuse you no matter what I feel," Peter said.

"Even at my age, Mr. Styles, I enjoy flattery. Thank you."

He wondered what her age might be? She looked an extremely vigorous and well-preserved sixty. It occurred to him that she might well be years older than that.

She looked down across the lawns toward the jumping course where yesterday Rex Barton had abruptly ceased to be. "You haven't had much chance to see Marlingham, have you?"

"Not much, I'm afraid."

She turned to look at him steadily. "You came on an unhappy accident the moment you arrived, and I'm told you were taken ill last night."

"You were told I passed out on three martinis, weren't you?" Peter asked.

"That story is going the rounds. Also another one."

"Oh?"

"It's being said you were drugged."

"I see."

"Were you?"

"I have no medical proof of it, Mrs. Moffet. I can only say that three martinis aren't usually a problem."

"I should have thought not," Clarissa Moffet said. Once more her glance strayed off over the beautifully cared-for grounds. "I came here to Marlingham as a bride, Mr. Styles, fifty-six years ago." She chuckled. "I saw you struggling with my age a moment ago. I was eighteen when Leonard Moffet—the fourth Leonard Moffet—brought me here and it became my home. For fifty-two years Leonard and I shared it together. Fifty-six years ago, Mr. Styles, owning and living in such a place as Marlingham was not unheard of. There were many estates as elaborate and expensive to maintain scattered around the country. Taxes weren't what they are today. A wealthy man—and Leonard was very wealthy—could manage without pinching. Times have changed." Her eyes clouded.

"When Leonard died four years ago, I found myself in the position of being unable to keep Marlingham going for very long. You've probably heard from Bill Tompkins that I've had opportunities to cut it up like a pie and sell it piece by piece. If I were willing to do that, Mr. Styles, I would be a comfortably rich woman with an income sufficient to do anything that most people in the world would ever want to do. But I am not most people. Marlingham has been my whole life. The one tragedy in an otherwise rich and deeply happy marriage was that Leonard and I could not have children. Marlingham became the center of our lives. We lived here, we entertained here—the famous and the infamous. Every stick of furniture, every painting, every tiny *objet d'art,* every shrub and flower and tree, are precious to me. I am not a religious woman, Mr. Styles. I'm a materialist who cherishes material possessions. I have clung to Marlingham by every single means at my disposal, every financial trick. I've even prayed to a God I don't believe exists. Somewhere there is somebody who can afford Marlingham, who will want it as much as I want it and love it as much as I love it. Until that person appears on the horizon, I've got to hang on to Marlingham. I will not see it split up, divided, turned into a country club or a hotel. After I am dead I won't know what happens to it, but while I live it has got to be preserved." She tossed her cigarette away onto the grass. Her voice had grown urgent and tense. Now she smiled. "Do I sound childish to you, Mr. Styles?"

"Not childish."

"But I don't make sense?"

"I think I can understand how deep the roots are," Peter said.

She was silent for a moment. "Then you'll understand why I've leased the place to Montague Spain. To me it means I can hang on for at least another two—possibly three—years. But there are things I hadn't anticipated, Mr. Styles."

"Oh?"

"Have you seen this morning's paper?" She reached down, shifted the cut flowers in her basket, and came up with a copy of a New York tabloid.

On the front page was a studio portrait of Rex Barton. Peter was startled to realize that for the first time he knew what Barton looked like. He'd only seen him with the clown makeup on his face. There was a brief caption under the picture indicating Barton had been killed in a riding accident at Marlingham. "Details on page 3."

On page 3 was a panoramic photo of Marlingham, obviously taken from the paper's morgue. Under it was a brief account of the finding of Barton with the clown makeup on his face. Peter found himself featured as the discoverer of the body. This was followed by a rehash of what had been appearing in gossip columns for the last month—the scandalous bits about Carol and Mark Fleming; past history about Carol and Orrin Pell. There was a picture of Carol in a passionate embrace with Pell, taken from some early movie.

Barton was forgotten—used as an excuse to revive all the juicy items in Carol's career.

"It's like having someone write dirty words on the walls of your living room," Clarissa Moffet said sharply.

"Carol must be burning," Peter said.

Clarissa Moffet turned her head. "You know her personally?"

"Grew up with her," Peter said.

"I guess I've put my foot in it," Clarissa Moffet said.

"Of course you haven't. I hadn't seen Carol, until two days ago, since she was fourteen. But I'm not sure I see what you're leading up to, Mrs. Moffet. What is it you think I can do for you?"

She looked away down over the lawns again. "It's a curious thing, Mr. Styles, but I find myself falling into an attitude that I bitterly resent in the world today. Everyone feels that they are entitled to something. Entitled to jobs, entitled to living space, entitled to security, entitled—entitled to paint faces on dead bodies if they feel like it! In my day we *earned* the right to work, we *earned* the right to live where we chose, we *earned* our security. We weren't free to make public spectacles of ourselves, and if we did, we didn't profit from it. Your friend Carol Richmond is, I understand, getting seven hundred and fifty thousand dollars for making this one picture. This entitles her to make her love life into a public *hors d'oeuvre,* the tidbit devoured before every cocktail hour. She's entitled to capitalize on her amoral code of living. She is entitled to make a public ninny of her husband, and in effect to invite the world to watch what goes on in her bedroom. For all this she will probably get a million dollars for her next picture."

"Just in passing," Peter said, "she's a good actress."

"Perhaps," the old woman said, almost passionately, "but not a good person. Because she feels entitled to be public with her life, she changes the attitudes of millions of dissatisfied women all over the country. She creates an evil climate, Peter, just as the gangsters of the bootleg days became public heroes and are still being glorified on our television screens. They were, they thought, entitled to break a foolish law. We haven't shaken off the climate of lawlessness they created. Our country doesn't *look* the same or *feel* the same because people assume they are entitled to live as they choose, without regard to code or tradition."

"In very broad terms I agree," Peter said. "I don't think I blame someone like Carol, though. It's the women who use her as an excuse who are the problem in my book. They create the climate in which *she* lives, not the other way around. In 1963 the President was assassinated. I don't blame the psychotic unfortunate who pulled the trigger nearly as much as I blame the community where by reckless slander, bigotry, and meaningless hatred a climate was created in which Lee Harvey Oswald thrived. The problem in my book is what to do about our society at large, and not what to do about the results of their attitudes. Cure the disease, not the symptoms."

"You call the perverted sense of humor that would paint a clown's face on a dead man a symptom?" Clarissa Moffet asked.

And on an unconscious live man? Peter asked himself. "There has to be someone to laugh at a joke or it's no fun," Peter said.

"To laugh at it—or to be frightened by it?"

Peter looked at the old woman sharply. "Frightened?"

"Apparently you and the police and everyone else thinks it was some kind of bad joke, Peter. I've wondered, from the moment I heard about it, if it might not be a warning."

"Warning?" If so, Peter thought, he had been warned himself.

"You don't have to peep through keyholes or have your ear to the ground to hear the rumblings of a coming explosion here at Marlingham. When people smash all the codes and enjoy what we old-fashioned folks think of as evil, there is usually some zealot around who decides to take the law and the punishment into his own hands."

"What had Rex Barton done? He had no friends here except Louis Beaujon, who gave him his job. He was a loner."

"I don't know," Clarissa Moffet said, "but it might be worth trying to find out, don't you think?"

"I think," Peter said gravely, "that you've reminded me I haven't been thinking of this as a reporter. But you still haven't come to the favor you wanted to ask."

Clarissa Moffet took the newspaper up from the bench and dropped it in the basket with her flowers. "I told you that I found myself falling into an attitude that I resent in other people. I feel *entitled* to keep Marlingham from having a clown face smeared over its public image. I don't want it remembered as the place where Carol Richmond went to bed with Mark Fleming. I don't want it remembered as the place where jealousy and hatred and perversion created a scandalous explosion. I want it remembered as the home of the Moffets, where in the past century Presidents were house guests, where the great intellects and the great artists of our age gathered and were nourished. I want it remembered for its beauty and for a graceful way of life."

"And you think I can help?"

She looked at him earnestly. "You may be the only person who can, Peter. You're here to write a story about the making of what they call an 'epic.' I know your career and the kind of thing you do. You're not here to augment the gossip columnists and the writers for the fan magazines. You're here to do an intelligent and civilized piece on something that has become a part of our way of life. What you write will be read by people who matter."

Peter laughed. The real reason he'd come here was to answer a cry for help, and he still hadn't heard from Carol what kind of help she needed. "I'm not quite sure how what I do can help you," he said.

"In spite of what's happened and will happen here," she said, as if she hadn't heard him, "you could preserve Marlingham's real image, at least for the future." Her eyes flickered and there was a kind of pained anger in them. "I'm in what your friend Bill Tompkins called 'a bind.' In my desperate anxiety to save Marlingham I have, by leasing it to Montague Spain, placed its very existence in danger. A Marlingham remembered only for excesses is not Marlingham. A Marlingham remembered for promiscuous women, and drunken men, and jokers who paint comedy masks on the dead is not Marlingham. You could stop all that, Peter."

"My dear lady, how?"

"The power of the written word, the public statement, is the one thing these people fear. Watch, Peter. See what there is to see and write about it. Montague Spain is an evil and cynical man, but he's got millions of dollars at stake here. He can stop all this bawdry, all this sensationalism in an instant if he chooses. The cheap little gossip columnists and feature writers are grist to his mill. But you could stop him cold if you chose to use your skills, your integrity, to show your audience the real picture of this decadent rabble!"

Peter reached out and covered one of her cool white hands with his. "I promise you what I write will be a true story," he said.

"Bless you," she said. She picked up her basket of flowers and rose from the bench. "I'm living in the golf professional's cottage at the foot of the west lawns. Please come to see me and let me help you."

"It'll be nice not to have to look for an excuse," Peter said, "because I'd come anyway."

The gray eyes danced. "I believe the modern phrase for that is 'sweet talk,' Peter."

Peter watched the old woman, her body erect, her step firm, move down across the lawn toward the big house. "*It's like having someone write dirty words on the walls of your living room,*" she'd said. Monty Spain would have laughed uproariously if he'd heard that. He would have thought of it as an antique sense of the fitness of things. There was something unreal about it, and yet touching. Clarissa's world, a small private world, was tumbling down around her. But weren't we all in the same boat? The rules, the traditions, the etiquettes, all the little safety islands of another age had disappeared, obscured by the shadow of sudden and total destruction. Why not live for the moment, for its immediate pleasures? And in the wild race to nowhere we must classify hatred, and bigotry, and violence as forms of pleasure. To hate a communist, or a Negro, or a politician of the other party, or a neighbor for what he has that we don't have, is a method of justifying—just in case there *is* a God waiting to pass judgment once we've destroyed ourselves with our self-made instruments of death.

Turning away from Clarissa Moffet was like turning back into a new world; away from a world of relaxed and gracious living to a world of intrigue, and jealousies, and vicious humors.

The face-slapping scene was apparently over. On the terrace Carol and Mark Fleming had moved onto the scene of action and were being carefully placed, a cameraman ordering chalk marks on the flagstones for them. Sherry Garth and Orrin Pell had moved off to one side and seemed to be engaged in some sort of rather heated conversation. Francis X. Garrity sat slumped in his canvas armchair. He looked almost as if he'd fallen asleep, but Peter saw that he never took his eyes off Carol.

As he stood there watching, Peter saw a woman coming toward him with a purposeful manner. He recognized her as Carol's maid. He moved away so that he was hidden from the terrace by a clump of lilacs. If Carol was sending him some sort of message, there was no point in attracting Garrity's attention.

The woman had seen him move and she came directly to where he waited. She was middle-aged, with a lined, worried face. Her eyes never met Peter's directly.

"Madam asked me to bring you this note, sir," she said, and handed him a small, folded piece of paper.

"Thanks." Peter took the paper and unfolded it. There was a scrawl on it in Carol's schoolgirl handwriting.

At the lunch break I'll get rid of Francis and come to your room. *Please* be there. Carol.

Peter looked up. The maid hadn't waited for an answer. She was headed for the house. Peter smiled. It was typical of Carol, he thought, that she wouldn't expect an answer. A summons was a summons.

Peter glanced at his watch. It was a little after eleven. The lunch break would be at least an hour away. One thing that had stuck in his mind from his conversation with Clarissa Moffet was her suggestion that the clown-face painted on Rex Barton had been a warning, not a joke. What Clarissa didn't know was what he'd seen when he looked into his own mirror that morning. If it wasn't the work of a haphazard joker painting obscenities on the handiest wall, then it had to mean there was some connection between Peter and the dead actor. There was only one possible thing they could have in common: a relationship with Carol. He would ask Carol, when they met, what role Rex Barton might have played in her past.

Peter was interested to see Carol and Mark Fleming work together. These two were the ingredients of explosion, from all accounts. He moved a little closer to the terrace.

The scene was being paced out for the cameramen. It seemed to consist of a very brief moment. Carol, in one of the wicker armchairs, was reading a magazine, apparently restless. She kept glancing toward the end of the terrace. Finally, with a little gesture of impatience or irritation, she threw down the magazine, stood, and started for the house. At that moment Fleming appeared on the far end of the terrace. He called to her. She turned, and even at a distance Peter thought he could almost see her trembling with excitement. Fleming came quickly across the terrace and took her in his arms. This was only a walk-through of the blocking for the scene, but that embrace was suddenly so passionate, so real, Peter thought he could hear a soft, shuddering sigh from the dozens of onlookers. When they finally broke apart, Carol and Mark stood looking intently at each other. The spell was broken by one of the camera crew who asked them to step aside while he made his chalk marks on the terrace. Fleming turned away, hands jammed into his pockets, and walked briskly to the end of the terrace. Carol, trancelike, went back to her chair and took her place with the magazine again.

"Dry run," Louis Beaujon said through the loudspeaker.

Spain looked asleep, white hat pulled down over his eyes.

There was no such thing as a "dry run" between Carol and Fleming, Peter thought. The brief moment of rehearsal had left him feeling uncomfortably stirred. That, he told himself, was the "chemistry of star combinations" which, according to Bill Tompkins, made the banks shell out huge sums of money. No doubt it was there—the chemistry.

4

STILL FEELING a little rocky from his night's experience, Peter decided to go back into the house for another cup of coffee.

The breakfast room had been stripped of the morning supply of food. Only the silex coffeepot remained, with cups and saucers standing by on a silver tray. Peter helped himself and lit a cigarette. His attention was attracted by a painting over the mantel he hadn't noticed in the earlier morning fog. It was one of Thomas Hart Benton's grim Midwestern landscapes, with the stooped and gnarled figures of a man and woman in the foreground. The toilworn couple in the painting were an odd contrast to the brittle glitter of what was going on out on the terrace.

The low angry voices of a man and woman in argument distracted Peter's attention from the painting. As he turned away, Sherry Garth came into the room, trying to wrench free from the firm grasp Orrin Pell had on her arm. Both of them wore black glasses, badge of the trade.

"Well, Peter!" Sherry said. She sounded relieved.

Pell slowly loosed his hold on the girl's arm. He was smiling, but it wasn't pleasant.

"I saw you on the terrace for a while," Sherry said, crossing over to the coffeepot.

"Getting a look at how it's done," Peter said.

"Nothing very interesting this morning," Sherry said.

"Unless you count an abandoned moment between our stars," Pell said. His voice was low, cultivated, and yet it had an unpleasant, sardonic edge to it. He'd made his reputation playing heavies in the films, and evidently his technique carried over into real life. His black glasses fixed on Peter. "I had a feeling you wouldn't be able to see anything very clearly this morning, Styles."

"You two have met?" Sherry asked.

"I guess we know who each of us is," Pell said. As he started for the coffeepot, Sherry moved quickly to Peter. It was quite plain she wanted no contact with Pell.

"I saw you talking to old lady Moffet out on the lawn," Pell said. His laugh was unpleasant. "The witch of Endor!"

"I found her very pleasant," Peter said.

"A creep," Pell said angrily. "She's supposed to be segregated in the golf pro's cottage, supervising the ground crew—the care of the outside of the place. But you'll stumble on her wandering around the big house at twelve or one o'clock in the morning, touching the walls as though they were the flesh of her ancestors. God, how she hates us! Yesterday I caught her going through my bureau drawers. She muttered something about something personal she'd left behind. She's determined to get something on any of us, all of us!"

"I'm afraid we all seem a little garish to Mrs. Moffet," Sherry said. "But she puts flowers in my room. I can't hate her for that."

"Puts flowers in, and probably reads your mail!" Pell said.

"I haven't had a chance to thank you properly," Peter

said to Sherry.

"Someone had to behave like a human being and help you," she said.

"That didn't require you to speak up in my defense," Peter said. "I understand you risked The Monster's wrath by suggesting he'd drugged my drink."

"It was obvious," she said. "Monty never lets anyone get away with insulting him."

"And he's not going to let you forget, either, baby," Pell said. "That crack about the garment district was just the beginning. He pulls another one like that and I'll knock his teeth down his fat throat."

"Don't play the hero, Orrin," Sherry said. "It doesn't suit your style. You know nobody knocks Monty's teeth down his throat and goes on working in the picture business. So he'll rub my nose in it, but if I don't react to it, he'll get tired of it in a while."

"You really think somebody slipped you one, Styles?" Pell asked.

"If you'd waked up with my head this morning, you'd think so," Peter said.

"I've seen strong men take a dive under the local martini treatment," Pell said.

"So I've been told—over and over," Peter said.

Pell shrugged and turned to Sherry. "Want to rehearse that next bit for a while before lunch?"

"No, Orrin."

Pell gave Peter a little twisted smile. "I leave the field to you, pardner." He gave Sherry a mocking bow and left them.

"Bastard!" Sherry whispered, under her breath. "Give me a cigarette, will you, Peter?"

He offered his case and lighter. "Seriously, I can't thank you enough for last night. I don't think I could have made it under my own steam."

"I grew up a girl scout," she said.

"When you left me last night—I was asleep?"

"Out like a light," she said.

He hesitated. "You know about my leg?" he asked quietly.

The black glasses turned sharply his way. "Doesn't everybody who reads the papers? I must say you handle it well. I have no idea which one it is."

"You didn't take it off after I'd passed out last night?"

She stared at him, her mouth open. She sounded angry when she spoke. "What on earth makes you think I'd be guilty of such an invasion of privacy?"

He smiled. "A girl scout might have thought I'd be more comfortable."

"My good Samaritanism doesn't go that far, my dear Peter."

"My artificial leg was off and placed on the floor beside my bed when I woke this morning," Peter said casually. "I haven't the faintest recollection of doing it myself. I wondered."

"It would never have occurred to me," she said.

"Somebody came into the room after you'd gone, then," he said.

"You probably did it yourself and have simply forgotten," she said. "You were in a deep fog."

"I think not," he said. "You can imagine how curious I am to know who came into the room after you'd gone and paid me such intimate attention."

"No one's spoken to you about it?"

Peter shook his head.

"Isn't Francis Garrity's man Marshall assigned to take care of you?"

"I talked to Buck this morning. He said he was on his

way up to offer help but that you told him I was all right."

She nodded, frowning. "That's true. I met him at the foot of the stairs when I came down from your room. He'd heard and was on his way up. I told him you were out cold and that the best thing was to let you alone to sleep it off."

"It gives you an odd feeling to know that someone was pawing you over while you were unconscious," Peter said.

"A horrible feeling," she said with a little shudder. "I couldn't lock your door, Peter, when I left you. There's no lock on the outside. Only a bolt on the inside."

"I know."

"If someone meant to do you a favor—make you more comfortable—why keep it a secret?"

He had no intention of telling her that there'd been much more to it than the removal of his leg. "Anyway," he said, "my deepest thanks to you for what you did do. Anytime I can repay the favor, let me know."

"If you mean that it may come sooner than you think—if Orrin doesn't keep his hands off me!" she said angrily. "Why is it only the heels get interested in me?"

Peter smiled at her. "Not only the heels, Sherry. The heels may have an unpleasant way of showing their interest, but the rest of us—?"

"Buy me a drink sometime and tell me what a nice girl I am," she said. "I need to be told sometime by someone who isn't simply interested in making a pass at me."

"That's asking a lot," Peter said, "but I'll make a bold try whenever you say."

In his room Peter lay down on his bed to wait for the luncheon break and the visit from Carol. Whatever it was they'd put in his drink last night, it had left him feeling bruised and aching as though he'd been beaten with clubs.

The aspirin had eased the pain in his head. But the passage of time, the casual conversations he'd held, had done nothing to relieve the fierce, throbbing anger he felt at having been, literally, violated in his unconscious state. He had called it an "odd feeling" to Sherry Garth. It was a simmering rage. The discovery that he'd been "handled" had brought back feelings of shame about his leg that he thought he'd lived down a long time ago. He wondered what thoughts his nocturnal visitor had had when he saw the stump of the leg with its flushed, pink flesh? What comments, if there'd been more than one? Had they laughed at him? They could have felt nothing but contempt for him in his helplessness.

Peter lay there on his bed, his eyes closed, his fists clenched at his sides. Sooner or later someone was going to pay for that period of pleasure. It was a moment which he would never forgive or forget.

He hadn't thought too clearly about the approach to it. There was no way to get on the trail without asking questions of a lot of people—perhaps all the people who had access to the house. The minute he started on that tack, the entire population of the Black Glass City would know that he'd been visited while he was in a helpless stupor. He hated to reveal it. He dreaded the amused speculations about it. His personal privacy was his most precious possession. If he told his story outright, he would open himself to the kind of lewd wonderings that follow a girl who's been raped.

There was a knock on the door.

"Just a minute," Peter called out.

He got up from the bed and went to the bureau, where he brushed his rumpled black hair. Then he went to the door and slid back the bolt.

It wasn't Carol. Francis X. Garrity stood there, looking calmly at Peter through his owlish glasses. He held a long, thin cigar between his square fingers.

"Carol's not coming," he said.

"She sent you to tell me that?" Peter asked.

"Not exactly. But she knows I'm here. I told her I was coming. Could we not do our talking in the hall?"

"This is getting to be a joke," Peter said. "Come in. I agree it's high time we did a little talking."

Garrity walked past Peter into the room and Peter closed the door and slid the bolt into place again. Garrity had gone to the windows and was looking down over the lawns, his back to Peter.

"Carol told you she'd made an appointment with me?" Peter asked.

"Emily is on my payroll," Garrity said, without turning.

"Emily?"

"Carol's maid."

"That must make it just dandy for Carol," Peter said. "Her maid spies on her; your jack-of-all-trades, Marshall, spies on her. There are others?"

"Oh, yes," Garrity said, without emotion.

A nerve twitched high up on Peter's cheek. "I think I was wrong," he said. "I can't imagine what we could possibly have to talk about. Unless you think that this was to be a lovers' meeting between me and Carol."

Garrity turned. He was smiling faintly. "My dear fellow, I had no such idea. It would almost certainly occur to Carol, but not to you. I know your kind. You play the game by rules that almost everyone else has forgotten. I find it refreshing—and comforting."

"I find myself revolted by a man who hopes to save his marriage by setting up his own Gestapo," Peter said. "Carol came to see me in New York the other day because, she says, she's in some kind of trouble. Frankly, that's why I came to Marlingham. Thanks to having been slipped a mickey last night, I haven't had a chance to talk to her and find out what that trouble is. She was coming here now to tell me."

"Did Carol also tell you that I might be the cause of her trouble?" Garrity asked.

"She did."

"Well, I'm not," Garrity said. He turned his cigar around in his fingers and then took a deep drag on it. He tilted his chin and blew the smoke up toward the ceiling. "If you'd invite me to sit down, and if you had a drink you could offer me, I'd like to tell you what Carol's trouble is and why I don't want you to involve yourself in it."

Peter glanced at the bureau. The bottle of bourbon Buck Marshall had brought him on his arrival yesterday stood there, its seals unbroken.

"Bourbon and tap water is the best I can do." Peter said.

"Please," Garrity said. He looked suddenly old and tired.

Peter discovered that a wide-mouthed thermos jug on the bureau contained ice cubes. Marshall's inadequacies as a houseman did not, it seemed, cover his actual physical duties. Peter made Garrity a drink and took it to him. He had to admit that curiosity outweighed his distaste for the man.

Garrity took a sip of the drink and glanced at the chintz-covered armchair by the windows. "May I?"

"Help yourself."

Peter took the straight chair by the bed, turned it around and straddled it, his arms resting on the back. He waited in silence. Garrity took another sip of his drink and carefully flicked the ash of his cigar into the silver tray on the little table beside the armchair.

" 'Tale told by an idiot,' " he said. "About the only thing I'm an expert on, Styles, is me. So I have to begin with me. I'm sixty years old. I was born that long ago in a miserable little manufacturing town in Illinois. I had no education after the eighth grade except what I picked up in home study. From the time I was fifteen, I worked in all my free time at a machine in one or another of the local factories. I didn't have any future, or any particular ambition, or even any indignation at the kind of treadmill I was on. It happened to hundreds of guys around me. I didn't feel any different, or any more put-upon, than anyone else. My parents died in a movie theater fire when I was nineteen. So I was alone from then on. I used to go to the Class C baseball games on Sundays. Once I traveled to Chicago on a Sunday and saw the White Sox play the Yankees. The White Sox had been torn to pieces by the gambling scandal, but the Yanks had Babe Ruth and Bob Meusel, Waite Hoyt and Bob Shawkey, and a lot of other big names. That was the biggest day of my life until I was thirty years old. Oh, I saw movies. When I was a little kid I was in love with Norma Talmadge." Garrity's laugh was dry. "I never dreamed I'd see a movie star for real."

Garrity drew a deep breath. "I was working in a bottling plant at the time—when I was thirty. I came up with a new fast way for capping bottles after the carbonated soft drinks had been put in them. I was no engineer, you understand. It was just a common-sense notion. An old-timer at the plant persuaded me to have my idea patented before I showed it to anyone. I did—and suddenly everyone in the soft drink and the brewery business wanted to use my patent. One month I was making forty-eight dollars and seventy cents a week. The next mouth I had a hundred thousand dollars in cash for the preliminary leases on my patent. That was in 1934. Since then I'm like the guy in mythology. The king?"

"Midas?"

Garrity nodded. "No matter what I do with money, it comes back double. And still I was all alone. I had a chance now to belong to clubs, to own the finest house there was, to do anything a man could want to do. The only thing was I didn't have a taste for anything. My office was in New York now, and I bought a season box at the Yankee Stadium. I saw all the good ones come and go—DiMaggio, Gehrig, Ruffing, Gomez, Henrich, Combs, Keller, Red Rolfe—all of them. That was about all. That and the movies. I'd go to Radio City or to one of the little neighborhood houses, I guess, every day. I saw how people dressed, and I got myself a good tailor. I saw what good manners were, and I actually found some old dame who taught how to behave straight out of Emily Post. I took the course. I was ready to move above the machine shop level but I didn't have any place to move.

"Then one night, in a little theater over on Lexington Avenue, I saw Carol for the first time in a movie. She was dynamite. I guess you know that. For me it was like something over again; like when I was a kid with Norma Talmadge. A dream romance. It was almost enough—but not quite. When I was a kid I never even thought of the possibility of actually meeting Norma Talmadge. Now it was different. I had the money to put myself in the position to meet anyone. It occurred to me one night when I was lying in bed that there was no reason at all why I couldn't get to know Carol Richmond."

Garrity's cigar had gone out and he put it carefully down in the ash tray. "I went about it slowly. I talked to a fellow in my bank and told him if ever some of the movie boys came around trying to finance a Carol Richmond picture, I wanted in. It was almost a year before it happened. When it did, I put up a million dollars for a picture. Just in passing, I don't mind telling you I made a two-hundred-per-cent profit on the deal. And I met Carol.

"It was legitimate now for me to go to California, and as

chief backer of the picture, to meet her. She treated me like you'd treat a guy who has a million dollars invested in your future. Nice but not intimate.

"I had plenty of time. I had nothing on my mind but Carol and I could wait. And I did wait. She was married to Douglas Teale then. The studio built it up as the big romance, the ideal marriage, all that stuff. Carol, they said, had finally found her dream man. She gave out interviews to that effect. Since I had nothing to do but watch, I knew this was strictly for public consumption. Carol and Doug Teale weren't happy. He was playing around, like most of the Hollywood boys do. I couldn't understand it. A fellow who had Carol didn't need anyone else.

"One night at a party there was a big blowup. Doug was pawing over some new young measurement girl. Carol blew her top and made a stormy exit. I was waiting for her with an offer to drive her home. She accepted, I guess because she thought it would make Doug mad to see she didn't have to go alone. Anyway, that was the beginning."

Garrity picked up his dead cigar, brushed the ash off it with his fingertip, and held his lighter to it. "No use making the story any longer than necessary," he said. "I had a series of dates with her after that. She was a big success, but she knew that in Hollywood you're only as big as the box office returns on your last picture. I figured she was running wild to keep herself in the public eye. The more guys she played around with, the more the public was interested in seeing her on the screen. I gradually painted a picture for her. A picture of security. What if she had a husband who didn't need her money or her success? What if she could pick her pictures, the stories she was to act in, without any fear of what would happen if they flopped? I loved her, but I wouldn't ask for any privilege except to be her home base, her anchorage. She'd never have to worry about money.

She'd never have to worry about failure. I'd never get in her way. I'd just be there. Well, she bought it. So did I."

"But it hasn't worked?" Peter asked.

"For two reasons," Garrity said quietly. "For her it was like an alcoholic marrying the guy from A.A on the assumption that would stop her craving for liquor. Of course it didn't. She was helpless when an attractive man came along—like Mark Fleming. She just can't help herself. So instead of being home base, I'm a guy in the way."

"The second reason?"

"I found out I'd been kidding myself," Garrity said. "I didn't want to be home base. I wanted to be Carol's husband with all the privileges and rights that title implies."

"So she's trying to get out, and you're hanging on with the aid of your spy system," Peter said, when Garrity didn't go on.

"Oh, no. No, no," Garrity said. "She's not trying for out, because she knows she can't make it. I won't let go. Sooner or later, sometime, she's going to need me and I'm going to be here." His voice lowered. "And if I'm having her watched, it's not because I hope to prevent a love affair with Mark Fleming, or you, or anyone else. Those things will happen. I wish they didn't have to be so public, that I didn't have to know about them. She's not being watched to keep that score."

"So why, then?"

"Someone is trying to do her in," Garrity said quietly. "Professionally, and that means, of course, in the long run as a human being."

"She said something like that to me," Peter said. "Adding that you might be the person behind it."

"She doesn't understand me," Garrity said. "She thinks, in spite of my assurances, that I must hate her for the way she lives, for her involvements with other men. That's the standard way the script reads. Jealous, vengeful husband. But I'm not that. I'm waiting as patiently as I can for my turn. But when she's in trouble, I'll help her with everything I've got."

"So let's get to the trouble, then," Peter said.

"Little things at first; little irritating things," Garrity said. "It began here at Marlingham."

"A month ago?"

"Just about. Someone stole her personal makeup kit out of our rooms. She uses a special kind of makeup prepared for her by a firm of chemists. She has a very delicate skin, and the ordinary products tend to produce skin blemishes. It was irritating because it takes a week or so to get a new supply delivered. Then she got a telephone message asking her to meet someone somewhere. It was from Fleming." Garrity's lips tightened. "She went to the meeting place and he didn't show. She was burning. But Fleming, when she confronted him, swore he'd never left any such message. A telegram took her into New York to have lunch with an uncle of hers of whom she's very fond. The uncle didn't show. It turned out he couldn't have sent the telegram because he was in Switzerland."

A joker at work again, Peter thought. The same joker who was amused by clowns?

"When they first started to work here," Garrity continued, "there were long sessions on the script with Monty Spain. He had many working notes, suggestions, definite instructions for each actor. Whatever else he may be, Monty is a real professional at his job—meticulous, detailed in his preparations. Carol's script was annotated from one end to the other with Monty's special instructions and suggestions for her. One night while we were at dinner someone went into our rooms and tore Carol's script to shreds, scattering the little bits of paper around the room like confetti." Garrity sighed. "None of these things is conducive to calm nerves in a highly temperamental woman."

"I should think not. And that's it?"

Garrity shook his head. "Up to then you could classify the whole thing as malicious mischief," he said. "Carol stormed and fumed, quite naturally, but she was angry, not afraid. Then the telephone calls began."

"Threats?"

"Yes. The time for the pay-off was close at hand. Have cash available—in six figures. That was the gist of it."

"Payoff for what?" Peter asked.

Garrity drew a deep breath. "There's the rub, as the fellow said. Whatever it is the caller has on Carol, she won't tell me. You see, about the time they began, she had begun to suspect me. We'd had a noisy brawl. She'd worked it out in her own mind that I was trying to get her to throw in the towel."

"What towel?"

"She knows that I look forward to the time when she'll quit picture making and settle down to being a wife."

"Is that your dream?"

"Of course. But a long time from now. A long time."

"But you think the caller does 'have something' on Carol?"

"Why else her panic?" Garrity took a fresh cigar out of his pocket and lit it. "It was about a week ago when she stopped taking me into her confidence. And it was just a week ago when it went beyond the bounds of mischief. Eventually there's going to be a good deal of horseback riding in this picture. Carol is no great horsewoman. She can ride a little. She's had to, often, in films. In this picture there are hunting scenes, a lot of jumping, and so on. A double will do the difficult stuff for Carol, but she'll have to do her own riding for close shots. All the actors who'll have to ride have been assigned horses, and in their spare time, like the unfortunate Barton, they rehearse what they're going to have to do.

"A week ago today Carol went out for a casual ride—with Mark Fleming. Her horse shied at something that blew across the path and she was thrown. She was thrown because her saddle slipped off the horse."

"Slipped?"

Garrity looked levelly at Peter. "The girth had been cut through so that it was only held by shreds of leather. It gave way. It wasn't worn, you understand. It was cut through."

Peter's mind jumped to Rex Barton. "Maybe Barton's fall wasn't an accident after all," he said.

Garrity shook his head. "My first thought. I checked. There was nothing wrong with Barton's equipment. His saddle didn't slip. He was just thrown."

"Go on," Peter said.

"Carol and Mark were jogging along a bridle path when she was thrown. If they'd been riding hard, she might have been killed," Garrity said. "After that she was really terrified. She wouldn't let me near her. I don't know whether there were more phone calls. She stopped confiding anything to me. When she took off for New York day before yesterday, I had her followed. I thought perhaps the moment for the 'pay-off' had come. But she didn't go to her bank. She went to the Cosmopolitan Club, was there for some time. Who she called or what she did there I don't know. Eventually she went down to Gramercy Park—to you. I didn't know it was you until I saw your name plate in the building foyer." His mouth tightened. "She'd gone to *you* for help."

"And you object?"

"No. That is, not that it's you, Styles. But it's a bitter pill to swallow that it should be anyone but me, her husband. I could protect her. I could surround her with an army of bodyguards if she'd let me, if she'd tell me all she knows. I *want* to protect her."

"And that's why you wouldn't let her come to see me now?"

"I wanted to talk to you first," Garrity said.

"Doesn't it seem likely that, in the circumstances, she might tell me things that she hasn't told you?"

Garrity's voice hardened. "It's altogether likely," he said. "But first I wanted to make certain things clear to you. I am not the cause of Carol's trouble. I love her. I will do anything in the world to protect her from danger. If you're intent on helping her, Styles, I don't want you wasting time imagining that I'm the villain of the piece. I didn't want you to think that Buck Marshall, and Emily, the maid, and others you may stumble across are acting as spies for a jealous husband. I'm concerned with Carol's safety, nothing else."

Peter got up from his chair and walked over to the window. Garrity sounded peculiarly genuine. "So are you going to let me talk to Carol now?" he asked.

"I wish it could be the three of us," Garrity said.

"Until she can be persuaded to trust you, Garrity, I doubt if that would get us anywhere."

"Then talk to her alone," Garrity said.

"What she tells me in confidence I won't repeat to you," Peter said.

"Even if she puts the finger on someone?"

"Even then, unless she gives me permission. She's got to be able to trust someone."

"Of course you're right." Garrity sounded very tired. He stood up. "There's no point in her sneaking in here to see you. Let me tell her you'll come to her suite in five minutes. All right?"

"Let her come here," Peter said. "Here she'll be sure her wires aren't tapped by your little army of watchers."

Garrity sighed. "Have it your way," he said. "It's tough to realize that she may tell you things that she won't tell me, when all I want in the whole world is to protect her and care for her."

"When we get to the truth about this, she may come to understand that," Peter said.

"I'll send her to you," Garrity said. "Thank you for listening so patiently." He went off down the hall toward the suite of rooms he and Carol occupied.

One thing was certain, Peter told himself as he waited by the windows. Carol's "trouble" was real enough. One little nubbin of Garrity's story stuck in the front of Peter's mind. The fake telegram from the uncle in Switzerland. It suggested that whoever was worrying at Carol was aware of the intimate details of her life. Only someone in that position would know of a favorite uncle whose telegraphic invitation to lunch would send Carol scurrying off to New York in immediate response. Garrity might be expected to know about the uncle. Fleming? Pell, who had once been close to Carol? Of course the uncle might have been a favorite topic of conversation with Carol. She might have told anyone.

"Styles!"

It was a loud cry from somewhere out in the hall. It jarred Peter. It was like a high, broken scream.

Peter turned and moved quickly out into the hall. For a moment he froze in the doorway. A few yards down the hall someone was crawling toward him on hands and knees. Once more the cry of his name—a cry like a wounded animal.

It was Garrity.

Peter reached him, bent down, took him by the arm and tried to lift the man's dead weight. Garrity turned his head. His face had a crooked look to it, as though he'd had a stroke.

"Carol!" he said in a hoarse whisper. *"Please!"*

Peter let go the man's arm and moved swiftly into the suite occupied by the Garritys. The first room was a sitting room and it was empty. Peter called out Carol's name and then moved through an open door into the adjoining room.

It was a bedroom.

It was a shambles.

The white counterpane of one of the twin beds was spotted with scarlet blotches. Stretched face down on the bed was the body of a woman, legs hanging off to one side. For one jolting moment Peter thought it was Carol.

And then he saw the big straw garden hat lying on the floor. His breath made a whistling noise through his teeth as he moved slowly toward the bed. Clarissa Moffet's white hair was smeared and matted with blood. Peter could see that the whole side of her head had been smashed in by a terrible beating with some heavy weapon. It no longer retained a human shape.

It was only then that Peter became aware that there was someone else in the room. He sensed it, or heard something subconsciously. He turned, quickly, toward the windows that looked out over the lawns.

"Carol!" he whispered.

She was standing by one of the long green curtains that hung from ceiling to floor, as if she'd been trying to hide behind it. Nothing in Peter's whole life had ever rocked him back so hard on his heels.

The front of Carol's white blouse and her tan gabardine skirt were smeared with blood. There was blood on her face, and a streak of it on her golden hair, as if she'd raised a bloody hand to push it back from her face. In her hand was a bloodstained silver candlestick.

Her mouth was distorted by a curious grimace, lips drawn back from her teeth in a kind of animal snarl. Black glasses, spattered with red, hid her eyes.

Peter found he couldn't speak. He took a tentative step toward this terrible specter.

"Don't come any nearer!" she said, lips writhing.

It was a voice Peter had never heard before.

"Carol!"

"No nearer!"

Her right hand lifted threateningly, gripping the bloodstained candlestick.

Part Three

1

VIOLENT DEATH was not a novelty to Peter. He had served two years in the Marine Corps during the hottest fighting in Korea. He had seen his own father, screaming in agony, burn to death in a flaming automobile. He had seen the butchered bodies of two murdered girls at Darlbrook ski lodge in Vermont less than a year ago.

Something about this moment of horror topped them all. Not more than an hour ago he had been talking with the gracious old woman who now lay mangled on the bed. No longer ago than that he'd seen Carol in her brief, passionate little scene with Mark Fleming. The woman who faced him now, brandishing a bloody candlestick, was not anyone he had ever seen before. Shock or an insane rage had left only the bare outlines of anything recognizable.

The atmosphere itself was poisoned by the sickish sweet smell of blood.

From behind him, Peter heard excited voices. Carol's blood-flecked glasses turned past him toward the door. Peter heard a muffled oath in French as he turned to see Louis Beaujon, his face chalk-white, staring with disbelief at what must have looked to him like an abattoir.

"Don't move, Beaujon," Peter heard himself say. Then forcing himself to appear completely relaxed, he walked straight toward Carol. For an instant he saw her knuckles turn white on the candlestick and then she began to sway, like a toppling tree. He caught her before she fell, her head lolling to one side. The candlestick made a soft thudding sound as it fell on the rug.

Beaujon was the right man for the moment. Peter remembered he'd served for some years in the French Resistance. He must not be a stranger to violence.

Kneeling, Peter held Carol's dead weight in his arms. He looked down at her face, smeared on one side with blood, with something like pity. God, what a climax!

"Can you take a look at Mrs. Moffet?" Peter asked Beaujon. "I don't think there's any chance—"

Beaujon made a sound that might have been a laugh. "Skull smashed in like an eggshell," he said. "What in the name of God made her do it?"

"We need a doctor and the police," Peter said. "Will you make the calls?"

"Of course. And Monty must be told. This is the end."

"End?"

"Of the picture, of course."

"Will you, for God's sake, call a doctor and the State Police and forget about your epic?" Peter said angrily.

"Sorry. Of course." Beaujon's voice turned lifeless.

"Wait," Peter said. "Can you post someone outside the hall door so that no one else comes in here?"

"There's an extension phone in the sitting room," Beaujon said. "I'll keep anyone out."

Peter looked down once more at the twisted, white face of the woman in his arms. For a moment he experienced a vivid recall of a day twenty years ago when he'd held her like this—young, exquisitely alive and full of promise.

"Carol!" he said softly.

With his left hand he reached up and gently took the black glasses off her face. Pale bluish eyelids, fluttering, closed out the sunshine—and the horror within the room. He could hear Beaujon's voice as he spoke rapidly to someone on the phone. Beyond that a babble of voices. Garrity must have spread the alarm. The whole population of the Black Glass City was about to descend on them.

It was difficult to find a proper balance point with his artificial leg, but Peter finally managed, and he stood up with Carol in his arms. He walked with her out into the sitting room, kicking the bedroom door closed behind him. Beaujon was just turning away from the phone.

"Both coming," he said. He moved toward the hall door and turned the key in the lock. "What are you going to do with her?"

"I didn't want her to come to in there," Peter said. "I'd like to get her out of here entirely. My room's across the hall."

Beaujon shrugged. "You can't keep it from them forever." He jerked his head toward the sound of voices.

"Nothing must be touched in the bedroom," Peter said. "We don't know yet what happened."

"Oh?"

"Do you?"

"I assume—"

"Don't assume," Peter said. He glanced at the hall door. "I'll run that gantlet. You keep them out of here."

"Right." Beaujon went over to the door and unlocked it. Excited voices rolled over them in a wave as he opened the door. "Out of the way!" Beaujon said sharply.

Peter, carrying Carol, went quickly out into the hall. Voices seemed to claw at him. He had a blurred vision of faces—the gnomelike Samuels, Mark Fleming, Pell, Sherry, the ghost of Francis X. Garrity being supported by Buck Marshall. It wasn't ten yards to his own door, but it seemed miles. He made it and carried Carol to the bed where he put her down gently. Then he moved quickly back to the door, closed it in Buck Marshall's grinning face, and slid the bolt home. He was sweating as if he'd been in a foot race.

He went back to the bed and took Carol's limp hands in his. They were frozen cold. He pulled a pale blue quilted cover up over her. Then he went to the bureau and poured a stiff hooker of bourbon in a glass. When he tried to get it down her, he found her teeth were clamped together like a vise.

Someone was pounding on the door.

"What is it?" Peter called out.

"It's Buck! Mr. Garrity wants in."

"Nobody," Peter said. "Not till the doctor's seen her."

"Look, Peter, he's her husband."

"When the doctor comes."

He wasn't quite sure why he denied Garrity the right to be with his own wife. Some instinct warned him that Carol should not come to in the presence of her husband. He sat on the edge of the bed, looking down at her pale, tortured face. It was hard to imagine her in a rage so violent that she would beat the fragile Clarissa Moffet to a pulp—go on beating her long after she was dead. That was certainly what had happened. The beating had gone on long after life had deserted the old woman's frail body. Why? He remembered Pell's remarks about Clarissa snooping through personal belongings. At the time he'd been inclined to reject it as fact. Could Carol have caught her going through her private things? Would that have provoked such a fierce, uncontrolled attack?

Outside Peter heard the squeal of brakes and the slamming of a car door. Someone had arrived at the front entrance in a hurry. He got up from the bed and walked over to the windows. A black sedan was parked below them with medical license plates on it. The doctor had made it in nothing flat. It turned out he lived just down the road.

Peter went to the door and waited. Voices were still high-pitched with excitement on the other side of it. A moment or two later there was a brisk knock. Peter opened the door to a youngish man with a brown crew cut, carrying a black bag. Buck Marshall, supporting Francis Garrity, was right behind him.

"I'm Dr. Graham," the younger man said.

Peter stood aside. The doctor went straight to the bed. Garrity, leaning heavily on Buck Marshall's arm, followed him in.

"You had no right to keep me out!" he said, his voice shaken. "How is she?"

"Unconscious."

"Oh, my God."

The doctor was already preparing a hypo. "Shock," he said. He glanced at Peter. "Somebody outside told me Mrs. Moffet has been killed." He read the answer in Peter's face. "I've known her ever since I was a kid! It's unbelievable. This woman did it?"

"We don't know who did it," Peter said.

"Don't we indeed! How else can it be read?"

Buck Marshall had lowered Garrity down in the arm-chair by the window and then quietly left the room. The doctor was swabbing at Carol's face with a piece of cotton dipped in alcohol. He looked at Peter, startled.

"This isn't her blood!"

"I know," Peter said.

The doctor muttered something under his breath and went on working on his patient. Peter walked over to the armchair where Garrity sat huddled, looking like a very old man.

"Exactly what happened?" Peter asked.

Garrity moistened lips that trembled. "I went to fetch her. To send her over here to you. You know?"

"And—?"

"She wasn't in the sitting room where I'd left her, so I went on into the bedroom." His eyelids batted behind the lenses of his spectacles. "There it was. Carol—and the woman."

"Carol was beating her?"

"Not then. She was bending over her, with—with that thing in her hand. What was it?"

"A candlestick. You spoke to her?"

"I—I think I let out a kind of yell," Garrity said. He shuddered. "She turned and looked at me and I—for a minute I couldn't believe it was Carol. Her face twisted—and the blood. Teeth bared like a—like a dog! She didn't say anything. She just stared at me. There was—blood on her glasses."

"Then?"

"I—came for you—yelling for you, I guess. I guess I must have been near to fainting. The room spun around like I was suddenly drunk, and I could feel cold sweat on my face. I fell, I guess, because I was crawling along on my hands and knees when I saw you." Garrity drew a deep breath. "The pressure on her has been terrible. I suppose something snapped inside her."

"Possibly. Did she know Mrs. Moffet? Had they any dealings?"

"I don't think so. Knew her, yes. We all knew her casually. She was in and out of the house and around the grounds."

"No trouble with her? Carol, I mean."

"What trouble? It was just a goodmorning-goodevening-hello thing. The old girl was crazy for flowers. She put flowers in our sitting room a few times. We both thanked her. What trouble?"

Peter remembered that Clarissa Moffet had had any thing but a high opinion of Carol.

"When you came up from the terrace for the lunch break," Peter said, "you and Carol went straight to your rooms?"

"Yes. That is, we stopped in the hall downstairs to talk to Louis Beaujon. Carol had some questions to ask him about the afternoon shooting. Then we came up, and I—I told her I knew about the note to you and that I was going to talk to you, not her."

"This was in the sitting room?"

"Yes."

"Did you go into the bedroom at all?"

"I?" The eyelids blinked behind the glasses. "No. No, I didn't. We had a brief—brief argument, and then I came directly over here to your room."

"Did Carol go into the bedroom while you were there?"

"I don't think so. No. No, she didn't."

Garrity had been in Peter's room for at least a half hour. Time for it all to have happened after he left. Carol alone in the sitting room.

The doctor's voice cut into Peter's thought. "I think she's coming around," he said.

Peter moved quickly over to the bed, with Garrity following him unsteadily. Carol's eyelids were fluttering and after what seemed a long time she opened her eyes.

"Peter!" she said. Then she turned her head slightly. *"Don't leave me alone with him, Peter!"*

"It's the doctor, Carol. Dr. Graham," Peter said.

"Don't leave me alone with Francis!"

There was a choking sound from Garrity. "Please, my dear. Please!" he said.

"Peter!" Carol's whisper was urgent.

"It's going to be all right," Peter said. What could he say? How could he reassure her?

Her eyes closed.

"I'm going to give her sedation," Dr. Graham said. "The police will want to question her, of course, but she won't be up to it for a while." He glanced curiously at Garrity. "Your wife is a long way from being herself, Mr. Garrity. It will be some time before anything she says has any real meaning."

"Thank you, Doctor," Garrity said.

The doctor turned back to his bag to prepare a second hypodermic.

"Peter!" The whisper from the bed was almost inaudible.

Peter bent down, so close that he could feel her breath on his cheek. "What is it, Carol?"

"Who did it?" she whispered.

Peter felt his muscles tense. He looked at her. The troubled eyes were eager for his answer. "I don't know, Carol. Don't you?"

Her eyes widened. "She was just *there,* Peter!"

The place was suddenly swarming with State Police, headed by Sergeant Tresh. He'd probably heard a dozen different versions by the time he appeared in Peter's room, his weathered face set in hard lines. Very briefly Garrity told his story of finding Carol in the bedroom with Clarissa Moffet's body. Peter carried on from there with his own version of answering Garrity's cry for help, finding Carol in the bedroom, and bringing her to his own room when she collapsed.

"When can we talk to her?" Tresh asked Dr. Graham.

"Be some hours."

"God, Doctor, couldn't you have waited?"

"She couldn't have talked to you. Not rationally."

She'd sounded rational enough, Peter thought, in her

brief exchange with him. He didn't mention it to Tresh.

"Ben Jacobs is going to blow his top," Tresh said. "Any reason we can't take her fingerprints?"

"I don't know the law," Dr. Graham said.

"Technical crew is in the other room now," Tresh said. "We need her prints to match against what they find. Yours too, Mr. Garrity. Conscious or not, I can place her under arrest and take her prints."

"My wife and I won't stand on technicalities," Garrity said. He sounded stronger. "If you need our fingerprints, take them."

"Who's going to stay with her?" Tresh asked. "You sent for a nurse, Doctor?"

"Not yet. I will at once."

"I'll station a man in here," Tresh said. "Get a policewoman as soon as I can. Meanwhile, the rest of you—out."

"You've got to let me stay with her," Garrity said.

"Sorry. You can make your pitch to Jacobs when he gets here. I'm not going to have her talking to anyone but us if she comes to."

"Who's Jacobs?" Garrity asked.

"County Attorney. Now everybody but the doctor out, please."

"I'd like to get my topcoat out of the closet," Peter said.

"Help yourself. But you're not going anywhere, Mr. Styles. And since you were in the room, we need your prints, too. The other guy who was there? What's his name?"

"Louis Beaujon."

"I think we'll use the library as an interrogation room," Tresh said. "Bring this Beaujon down with you and we'll take your prints there."

Ben Jacobs was a small, neatly made man with thinning sandy hair. A graduate of the Yale law school, he was believed to have a very bright future in state and possibly national politics. He wasn't happy about the situation he found himself in at Marlingham. You could handle a dozen small, difficult cases brilliantly and only your friends in the field knew how good you were. Miss one big one like this—a case that would get nationwide publicity—and no one would ever forget. Locally, Clarissa Moffet was a person loved and respected. The Moffet family had been the center of the local community for a hundred years. Carol Richmond, the apparent murderess, was world-famous. Let her get off the hook, if she was guilty, and you'd be marked "no good" for ever. He knew that the first hour or two of his investigation might spell the difference between success or failure. The State Police were good men, but he wished he had help more experienced in dealing with a major homicide.

On Jacobs' behalf it should be said that he could have passed the case on to one of his assistants, at least in the beginning. He was involved in another case when the word came to his office. If an assistant bungled the preliminary investigation, he could always alibi himself. It never occurred to him to protect his political future by ducking the big one.

Jacobs didn't ordinarily have stage fright at the beginning of a case, but his nerves were on edge with this one. All the country's communications and publicity mediums would be down on his neck before he was fairly started. By reputation he knew Monty Spain and Mark Fleming and some of the others, in addition to Carol. They'd all be fighting for a good press and to hell with the man who had to wrap up the package. Now, before this all began to take shape and work against him, Jacobs knew he had to make real progress. Nerves were still raw; people might say things now they wouldn't say later. If you could hit before a witness had time to decide on a course of behavior, you had a chance. "Don't waste time on the wrong ones in the beginning" was a professional axiom.

Jacobs' first port of call was the scene of the murder. Nothing had been moved or changed. Jacobs had grown up in Chadwick, and Clarissa Moffet had been a familiar figure all of his life. The sight of her battered body made him sick at his stomach. And angry—deep-down angry. As a kid, Jacobs had caddied for her on the golf course. He remembered her as a great lady, pleasant, humorous, never playing the phony. He had personally benefited from a scholarship set up by the Moffets which helped to take him through Yale and the law school. It was hard for him to stay detached and coldly professional as he viewed the violent destruction of a fine person. For personal reasons he wanted to nail this case down fast and tight.

He was then taken down the hall to where Carol lay in a drugged sleep, guarded by Trooper Childers and the doctor. Tresh was his guide. Jacobs stood looking down at the still white face on the pillow. He had seen it many times before on the screen. It created the odd illusion that she was someone he knew well.

"I understand the doctor cleaned her up some," Tresh said. "Her face and hair and her hands were all smeared with blood."

"Why, Doctor?" Jacobs asked. "Until we saw her, why?"

Dr. Graham shrugged. "I thought she was hurt. I was looking for a wound—an injury. It wasn't till I was well under way that I realized it wasn't her blood."

"Bitch!" Jacobs said quietly. "When can she talk?"

"Late afternoon. Early evening."

"That's just great!" Jacobs said. "By then they'll be wanting to make a television show out of this. Okay, Tresh, who have you got lined up?"

"The husband, Francis X. Garrity. He found her standing over the body and went for help. A writer named Styles who answered his call for help and ran into the room. The woman fainted when he approached her to take the candlestick away from her. He carried her in here."

"Styles?" Jacobs said. "Peter Styles? Feature writer for *Newsview?*"

"That's the guy."

"All we need is to have a reporter in on the case ahead of us," Jacobs said.

A reporter on the scene of a crime spells headache to the professional investigator. He'll keep things to himself, hoping for a scoop. He'll try to be ahead of the police in order to cop the glory of a successful solution for himself. Jacobs knew that Peter Styles had been involved in a murder case not too long ago, and nobody remembered the name of the policeman on that case. Only the glamorous Mr. Styles.

Well, it had to be faced.

"We'll take 'em in order," Jacobs said. "The husband first, then Styles, then this Beaujon fellow. In the library."

Montague Spain was making a speech. He stood on a bandstand in a corner of Marlingham's ballroom, white linen hat pushed back on his head, a cigarette burning perilously close to the fringes of his grizzled beard and mustache. His heavy lidded eyes were narrowed to angry slits.

The entire population of what Mark Fleming had called the Black Glass City was assembled in front of him. The sun, pouring through the west windows, glittered against dozens of pairs of black glasses, raised to look at The Monster.

"First I will say the proper things," The Monster said. "I am shocked by the brutal killing of Mrs. Moffet. She wasn't my favorite person, but no one should come to such an end. From what we know now, it would appear that Carol killed her." The narrowed eyes flicked from face to face as though he expected a denial to come from somewhere. No one spoke.

"I, for one," The Monster said, "will not accept that as a fact until it is proved to me."

"You need photographs of her in action, boss?" Ron Samuels asked, grinning.

"I need silence from you, Buster," Spain said coldly. "I repeat, until it is proved to me, I don't accept Carol's guilt. True, she was under pressure. True, she's a temperamental person—explosive. True, Mrs. Moffet had a way of invading people's privacy."

"She was a creep," Orrin Pell said.

"In her right mind Carol wouldn't hurt a fly," Spain said. "If she is guilty, it's a clear case of mental derangement at the time. But that doesn't do us any good."

"Now we come to the important part," Pell said. "Money."

"Shut up, Orrin," Mark Fleming said.

"Let us be realistic," Spain said. "We do come to money. Roughly a million and a half dollars have gone into this picture already. If Carol is guilty, we've had it. In half an hour the bankers and the big boys in Hollywood are going to be on the phone to me, wanting to know where they stand. I can't tell them until the authorities give us a yes or no on Carol. In the meantime other things can wreck us. Too goddamned much loose talk can wreck us!" Spain dropped his cigarette on the floor and crushed it under one of his espadrilles. "We're about to be swarmed under by every fancy-hatted gossip columnist, every reporter and snooper you can imagine. Sightseers are going to crawl over us like ants over a dead rabbit. All of us are going to be asked questions by people who have no real right to ask them. If we all answer with our own private theory and contribute our own tidbits of juicy slander, we'll be drowned under a mass of publicity no production can survive. I've called you together to say this. If you talk to no one but the police, and if Carol is cleared, as she will be—as she *must* be—you'll all still have jobs and we'll go on making this picture. If you behave like a bunch of blabbermouthed housewives gossiping over the back fence, we've had it." Spain's lighter flared as he lit a fresh cigarette. "I've got a long memory, friends. If we're polished off by loose talk, I'll know who did the talking. And there won't be anyplace you can walk, anyplace you can live in the motion picture business when I get through with you." He paused, waiting for a comment. There was none. "Any formal statements made to the press will be cleared through me. No comment is all you've got to say, understand? No comment." The narrowed eyes swept over the heads of the crowd toward the door. "You! I want to talk to you."

Heads turned to see Peter Styles standing in the doorway. He was filling his pipe from an oilskin pouch. There was a thin smile on his lips, and his face seemed to be paler than normal.

"You want to talk, talk!" he said.

"In private!" Spain thundered. It was said more to the others than to Peter. The crowd began to move toward the door and Peter stepped just inside the room to make way for them. Sherry Garth, Pell, and Fleming were together and they made for him. Fleming, he saw, looked really shattered. There were dark circles under his smoldering black eyes, and there was an unhealthy look to his skin.

"Can you tell us anything?" Sherry asked, her fingers closing on Peter's arm.

"Nothing you probably don't already know," Peter said.

"She's unconscious?" Fleming asked, his voice hoarse.

"Under sedation. She came to for a minute."

"How did she seem? What did she say?" Fleming asked.

It could be, Peter thought, that more than simple sexuality was involved in his feeling for Carol.

"Nothing that was helpful," Peter said.

"There's no doubt, is there?" Pell said.

"Doubt?"

"That she did it!" Pell said impatiently.

"Of course there's doubt," Peter said. "I shouldn't talk about it because I haven't given my evidence to the County Attorney. But I can say this much. Neither Francis Garrity nor I saw Carol strike Mrs. Moffet. She was standing over the body with what I assume was the murder weapon in her hand. But she could have come into the room, seen Mrs. Moffet lying there on the bed, attempted to help her. That would account for the bloodstains on her and her clothes. She could have seen the candlestick on the floor and picked it up. You don't think in police terms when you're in a state of shock. You understand I don't know that it was that way, but it could be. Until the fingerprint men and photographers and the other experts get through in that room upstairs—until the police prove otherwise—there's doubt."

"You'll help her?" Sherry asked.

"She's an old friend," Peter said. "I'll help her in any way I can, no matter what the answer is."

"Styles!" The Monster bellowed from across the room.

"Please," Fleming said to Peter, "keep me posted on how she is."

"Will do," Peter said. "The doctor says she'll sleep for some hours." He nodded and walked across the room toward Spain.

"You represent a prize headache to me," Spain said, as Peter joined him.

"If I didn't know you had a few million bucks squeezing at your gut," Peter said, "I'd resent your yelling at me."

"Let's play it with the gloves off," Spain said. "I'll be me, you be you. The person that's me yells when the heat's on."

Peter gave him a tight little smile. "Fair enough," he said. The Monster had a way of disarming you with his candor just when you were ready to tell him off.

"I need to know where you stand," Spain said.

"Meaning just what?"

"You're the only public voice here at the moment. There'll be a million of 'em later. You're also a key witness. What you say in print will carry more weight than anything anyone else writes about us. We've got money in telephone numbers at stake here. What are you going to do to us?"

"That's a funny kind of question," Peter said. "Whatever I do write—when and if I do write—will be the truth as I find it, as I understand it. Let me point out to you I don't write for a daily paper or a radio or television news department."

"You're a free lance. You can sell your byline to anyone."

"I'm not going to," Peter said. "Perhaps I can make this clearest to you by saying that I'm pretty well disqualified for the time being as a public commentator on this. Carol is my friend. We were kids together. She's asked me for help—before this happened and since it happened. So however it comes out, I'm on her team."

"What's your opinion? Did she do it?"

"I don't have an opinion yet," Peter said. "All I know is she's going to need help. She'll get it from me. So I'm not selling tidbits to anyone."

Spain heaved a monstrous sigh, his lungs a giant bellows. "You think they'll pin it on her?" he asked.

"The police always pounce on the most obvious answer," Peter said, "and ninety-nine times out of a hundred the obvious answer is the right one. At least until Carol is able to tell her own story it will look open and shut to the police. The County Attorney is the man who holds most of the answers. If he just wants a quick solution, he'll settle for Carol now. If he's a conscientious investigator, he'll use the time while he's waiting for her to be able to talk to check every other possibility."

"What other possibilities are there?"

"You've got a hundred people working here, Spain. There's a grounds crew, local people who were working for Mrs. Moffet directly."

"Fifteen, counting three stablehands."

"You see? Any one of your hundred people could have had a row with Mrs. Moffet without your knowing. It could be some kind of local quarrel, dating back to long before you and your people ever came to Marlingham. Right now it looks like Carol. She was stained with the old woman's blood, and she had the murder weapon in her hand. I saw that myself. But there are an infinite number of other possibilities."

"A plea of temporary insanity isn't going to do me any good," Spain said.

"It isn't going to do Carol any good either." Peter said. "Can you imagine her spending the next few years in a mental institution?"

Someone touched Peter on the shoulder and he turned to find Trooper Childers there.

"Ben Jacobs wants you in the library, Mr. Styles."

2

JACOBS SAT at a carved Florentine desk in the library, scowling at a stack of notes. He'd just finished his session with Francis Garrity. He was a chain smoker, and the bronze ash tray at his elbow was already beginning to fill up. To his right a young man sat at a stenotype machine, watching him.

Peter walked into the library prepared for almost anything, but not what first caught his eye. He hardly glanced at Jacobs or the male stenographer, because over the mantel, behind the desk where Jacobs sat, was an oil painting. It was the picture of a clown. He learned later that it was by George Luks, who had made a great reputation as a painter of circus figures. At the moment it struck Peter where he lived. The face on the canvas was an exact duplicate of the one he'd seen on a dead man and in his own mirror. The joker had found his inspiration here in Marlingham's library.

"You an art connoisseur, Mr. Styles?" Jacobs asked, in a crisp, impatient voice.

Peter took his eyes away from the painting. "Sorry. I hadn't seen it before. It gave me a jolt, because I saw a copy of it yesterday somewhere else."

"Rex Barton?"

"Yes. And I saw it somewhere else later."

"Where else?"

Peter glanced at the stenotype operator. The young man's fingers were poised over the machine. Peter drew a deep breath. "On my own face."

"How's that?" Jacobs leaned forward, his eyes bright.

Slowly, a little painfully, Peter told Jacobs of his experience the night before—the drugged drink, his waking with leg removed, and the vision that peered back at him from his bathroom mirror. "I haven't told this to anyone else," he said. "I thought it was a miserable kind of joke and I was sore as hell. It was my intention to catch up with whoever did it and give his perverted sense of humor a going-over. I've had no chance to follow up."

"Damndest thing I ever heard of," Jacobs said. "You don't have any personal enemies here?"

"The only person I've ever known at all is Carol Richmond, and I hadn't seen her since we were kids. I'd met her husband a couple of days ago."

"That was when Carol Richmond came to you for help?"

Peter's eyebrows lifted. "You know that?"

"I've just finished talking to Francis Garrity," Jacobs said.

"Then if he's told you his whole story, I have very little to add. Carol never got a chance to tell me about her troubles, thanks to my drink-drugging friend. All I know myself is from Garrity. The stolen makeup kit, the phony phone calls and telegram, the torn-up script, the cut saddle girth."

Jacobs nodded. "Those are the things he told me about." He hesitated. "You're not the usual kind of witness, Mr. Styles. You're a trained observer. You even have a small reputation in the field of crime. I'd like to know whether

I'm to regard you as a competitor, an ally, or strictly as Carol Richmond's friend."

"Nice point, nicely put," Peter said. "Let's begin with what I'm not. I'm not a competitor. I'm an ally in the sense that I won't lie to you or try to mislead you. But as of the moment I'm strictly Carol's friend."

"You don't think she did it?"

"I could be her friend if she did, couldn't I?"

"I like all your answers," Jacobs said. "That's rare in my business. Have you any reason to think she didn't do it?"

"Yes."

"Don't tell me yet," Jacobs said. He glanced at his notes, his eyes very bright. He fumbled for a cigarette. "You and Garrity were having a conversation in your room. You can tell me the details of that conversation later. He went back to his suite to send his wife to you. Right?"

"Right."

"Almost at once he came out into the hall screaming for help. You got to him first. Right?"

"Right."

"Take it from there."

A nerve twitched high up on Peter's cheek. "He whispered Carol's name to me," he said. "I thought something had happened to her. I went into the sitting room. Nobody there. Then I went into the bedroom. It—it was unbelievable."

"You saw Carol standing over the body?'

"No. I didn't see her at all at first. There was the body on the bed. For a moment I thought it was Carol. Then I saw Mrs. Moffet's garden hat, realized it was her. Some instinct made me turn and I saw Carol at the windows, smeared with blood, acting as though she was trying to hide behind the drapes. She—she had the candlestick in her hand. When I started to go to her, she told me not to come any nearer.

She raised the candlestick to use against me. It was apparent she didn't recognize me. Her voice was a stranger's voice. She was gone—way out gone."

"Then?"

"Beaujon came into the room. I told him to stand still and I walked toward Carol to take the candlestick away from her. Just as I reached her, she collapsed. I caught her as she was falling."

"You took the candlestick away from her?"

"No. She dropped it as she was keeling over."

"You didn't touch it?"

"No. I left it exactly where it fell. I don't think I touched anything in the room. I told Beaujon to clear the way for me—to call the police and a doctor. Then I picked Carol up and carried her to my room."

"Why did you do that?"

"I thought if she came to in that room, she'd really go off her rocker."

Jacobs frowned at his notes. "What in any of this makes you think she didn't do it?"

"I'm coming to that," Peter said. "She was still out cold when Dr. Graham arrived. In shock, he said. He gave her a hypo. Garrity was in the room by then. She came to after a while. The first person she saw was me. She spoke my name. No blank then. She whispered to me to keep him away from her—meaning her husband."

"Why?"

"She suspected he might be the person who'd been hounding her—the phone calls, all that stuff."

"Why?"

"She never got to tell me. Remember I'd had no conversation with her as to details. Garrity arrived at my apartment in New York as she was about to go into it. That was day before yesterday. I'd had no chance for a private talk with her since I got here. I don't know why she suspected her husband."

"Go on."

"She whispered my name again and I had to lean very close to her to hear what she wanted to say. I don't think the doctor or Garrity heard her. She said: 'Who did it?' "

"You're positive?" Jacobs asked sharply. "She didn't say, 'I did it!'?"

" 'Who did it?' she said. I said I didn't know and I asked her if she didn't. Then she said: 'She was just *there,* Peter.' "

"That's all?"

"That's all. By then the doctor and Garrity had come in close beside us and she didn't say any more. She just closed her eyes and seemed to go to sleep."

Jacobs ground out his cigarette in his ash-tray and lit another one. "You don't think she was faking?"

"No. She'd drawn a complete blank. She'd just come out of it. She obviously knew what had happened—that Clarissa Moffet was 'just *there.*' "

"She's an actress," Jacobs said.

"She was a woman in shock when I first saw her."

"She's an actress," Jacobs said stubbornly.

"That's my story," Peter said. "Until I talk to her again, I have to think those two statements from her were a moment of truth. We should be looking for another possibility while we're waiting for her to tell her own story."

"Damn!" Jacobs said.

"I'm sorry if I make it seem less cozy than you thought," Peter said.

"You think this clown face business has anything to do with the murder?" Jacobs asked. "Or is it just a separate joke?"

"I don't know."

Jacobs was silent for a moment. "When Garrity found

his wife, she was standing over the body with the candle-stick in her hand."

"But he didn't actually see her strike a blow. He told me."

"He *says* he didn't," Jacobs said. He was still fighting for an uncomplicated answer.

"Carol had been rehearsing a scene on the terrace just before the lunch break," Peter said. "She and Garrity came up to their suite. I asked him if he went into the bedroom. He says not. I asked him if Carol went into the bedroom before he left her to come to me. He says not. But after that, Carol obviously went into the bedroom. 'She was just *there,*' she says."

"You're suggesting the murder took place before they came up from the terrace. That the body was in the next room all the time?"

"If Carol didn't do it," Peter said, "it has to be that way. I know one thing. Mrs. Moffet was in the house. I had a conversation with her on the terrace about an hour before it happened. The last I saw of her, she was heading for the house with a basket of flowers. It was her habit to distribute flowers around the house."

"If it happened before the lunch break, your girl and her husband would be in the clear," Jacobs said, scowling.

"I can't vouch for it," Peter said. "But it should be easy to check out. I'd come up to my room to do some thinking and to lie down for a bit. I don't know of my own knowledge who came and went from the terrace. One thing should help you. A good part of the crew and the company were on the terrace, involved in rehearsal and actual takes. You should be able to eliminate three-quarters of the whole movie crowd. They had jobs to do and they were doing them."

"Thanks for small favors," Jacobs said. He turned to the

stenographer. "Ask the trooper outside to come in, Jerry."

Sergeant Tresh and Trooper Childers both came into the library. Jacobs, briskly efficient, told them it was his intention to check out all the other possibilities while they were waiting for the chance to talk to Carol. There was an hour's time to cover—from the time Mrs. Moffet left Peter to go to the house until she was found dead.

"Styles tells me a good part of the movie group were involved in shooting scenes on the terrace. A lot of them must have perfect alibis. Check out everyone you can."

Tresh looked surprised. "Is there any doubt the Richmond dame did it, Ben?"

"There's always doubt till we know for certain. I don't want anyone accusing us of missing any angles because we were too cocksure."

When the troopers went out, Jacobs turned to Peter.

"Satisfied?" he asked.

"I feel a hell of a lot better than I did when I came in here," Peter said. He grinned. "You could have been a heel."

"Don't get the idea I've bought anything," Jacobs said. He leafed through some papers on his desk. "I'll level with you since you've leveled with me. I have a preliminary report here from the homicide boys upstairs. There are only one set of prints on the candlestick—bold and clear."

"Carol's?"

"Yes."

"Well, no one's denied she handled it. I saw her with it in her hand myself."

"So you did."

"Just to try to keep you unhappy," Peter said. "Someone did try to harm Carol—physically harm her."

"The saddle girth," Jacobs said.

"Yes. The rest of the things could be called simple mischief. That was a direct effort to do her serious harm."

"The two things could have no connection." Jacobs scribbled a note on his pad. "One important question, Styles. You were talking with Garrity in your room. He left you to send Carol to you. You told me that 'almost at once' he came out into the hall screaming for help. How soon is 'almost at once'?"

"I have to play your side of the street to answer that honestly," Peter said. "Too soon for him to have gone into the bedroom, delivered that terrible beating which was not a matter of seconds, and come back out calling to me. And where was Carol while he did it? Seconds later I saw her in the room covered with blood. Garrity couldn't have done it." Peter's eyes narrowed. "Not then."

"When, then?"

"When you check out who was on the terrace and who wasn't, you'll know if he could have done it at all. He could have left the terrace while Carol was shooting her scene. I have no way of knowing whether he did or not."

Jacobs sighed. "The hell of this is we don't know whether the whole set of circumstances involved with Carol Richmond before this happened—the stolen makeup kit, the phone calls, the telegram, the destroyed script, *and* the saddle girth—have any connection at all with the murder. They could have no connection. They could have driven Carol to a state of mind where she blew her top at Mrs. Moffet without Mrs. Moffet having any connection with the other things."

"And the clown faces?"

"A completely separate joke."

"Or all these things are part of an elaborate pattern we don't see yet."

"I hope to God you're wrong. It all looked so simple when I first heard the facts."

There was a knock at the library door and Jacobs gestured to the stenographer. The young man went to the door and then turned back into the room.

"Jim Walters," he said.

"What's he want?"

"Got to talk to you, he says. Urgent."

"Bring him in." Jacobs turned to Peter. "You know Jim?"

Peter shook his head.

"Foreman of the ground crew Mrs. Moffet had here to take care of the place. Local man. Good guy."

Jim Walters was about forty, Peter guessed. He was a tall, sinewy, hard-muscled man with a brown, weathered face. He had dark eyes that were angry as he faced Jacobs across the desk. Peter might as well not have been there for all the attention he got from Walters.

"What happens to Mrs. Moffet now?" he asked.

"What do you mean?"

"What happens to her? Where do they take her?"

"The hospital," Jacobs said. "Autopsy."

"And all these people staying here at Marlingham?"

"How do you mean?"

"These movie bums," Walters said, almost fiercely. He gave Peter a contemptuous glance. He'd linked him with the "movie bums." "When do they get out?"

"As far as I know, Jim, they have a lease on the place. They can stay till the lease runs out. Whether they will or not depends, I should think, with whether they go on with the picture."

"None of us will work for them," Walters said.

Jacobs spoke patiently. "Look, Jim, I haven't got time for that problem now. I'm investigating a murder."

"The Richmond woman did it, didn't she? What's to investigate?"

"We're not sure yet. We haven't been able to question her."

Muscles rippled along Walters' jaw. "That *woman!* That whore!" His voice was unsteady. "I've worked for Clarissa Moffet since I was fifteen years old. A finer, decenter woman never lived. There's a lot of us want to be damn sure no one buys their way out of this one."

"You think someone's going to buy me, Jim?" Jacobs asked, his voice hard.

"They'll figure a way. She's worth too much dough to them. They'll get her off somehow."

"That's enough," Jacobs said.

"They've got to be gotten out of here," Walters said. "All of them. At least for the funeral. Clarissa's got a right to be buried from here, like all the Moffets before her, without these jerks standing around making jokes."

"That'll be up to the Moffet lawyers and the tenant. Get one thing clear, Jim. Nobody's going to 'buy' anybody. And we're not going to have any lynchings either."

"Whose side are you on?" Walters demanded. "Everybody knows Mrs. Moffet helped educate you. So whose side are you on?"

"I'm on the side of the law, Jim, and I've had about enough."

"Can I ask a question?" Peter asked quietly.

"This is Mr. Styles, Jim. He's a writer. He's had some experience with this kind of thing."

"I know all about him," Walters said. "Drunk the first hour he was here!"

"Do you know anything about a cut saddle girth, Walters?" Peter asked, keeping his tone quite casual.

"Yes, I know about it," Walters said. "I spent quite a lot of time trying to find out who was responsible. I've got two local kids working for me in the stable—Paul Miller and Eddie Teliskie. I guess you know them both, Ben."

"Know them and their families," Jacobs said.

"Aren't any of us in love with these movie bums,"

Walters said. "Highhanded know-nothings. Not the kind of people used to ride out of Marlingham's stables. I was afraid one of the boys had tried to get even with someone."

"You don't think they did?"

"I'm satisfied they didn't."

"You saw the girth after the accident? Saw it yourself?" Peter asked.

"Yes, Mr. Writer. I saw it. Cut through with something sharp as a razor blade. The boy should have noticed it when he saddled up. Eddie Teliskie it was. But they had him so goddamned rattled, changing saddles and all."

"Changing saddles?" Peter asked, his voice sharp.

"That woman—the Richmond dame—said she didn't like the saddle she'd been riding. Her boy friend—this Fleming—suggested she try his. He got Eddie to shift saddles."

"Wait a minute. These people always rode the same saddles?"

"Same tack. Same horse," Walters said. "They were supposed to get used to their equipment and the horse assigned to them so they'd be comfortable and familiar when they had to use them in the picture."

"Who would know what saddle belonged to who?"

"Marked in the tack room," Walters said. "Mr. Fleming, Miss Richmond—and so on. Label on each saddle rack."

"So that afternoon Miss Richmond rode Mr. Fleming's saddle?"

"That's the way it was, Ben. Fleming made Eddie shift saddles, adjust the stirrups, all that."

Jacobs glanced at Peter and then back to Walters. "It was the girth on Fleming's saddle that was cut?"

"Yes."

"So it was Fleming someone meant to take a spill."

"Looks like it, Ben."

"You didn't think this was worth reporting to the troopers?"

Walters shifted his feet. "I did and I didn't. I reported it to Mrs. Moffet. It was a sure thing one of my boys would be blamed for it. Fleming had thrown his weight around quite a lot. He wasn't liked. Then this Mr. Garrity came around investigating. He's the only decent one in the whole bunch. He said right off it was some kind of a bum joke, pulled by one of the movie bums. He said he'd handle it. So I let it lay there. Mrs. Moffet thought that was best."

"You told Garrity it was Fleming's saddle, not his wife's, that had been damaged?"

"He didn't ask me," Walters said with country simplicity.

The homicide specialists had finished their examination of the bedroom where Clarissa Moffet had died, and they came to report to Jacobs. Peter was excused, feeling relieved by what he'd found out about the County Attorney. Jacobs was alert, intelligent, and not trying to close any doors until he was convinced. Another kind of man in charge could have made things much, much worse.

"Don't get lost," were Jacobs' last words to Peter. "When we can question Carol Richmond, we may need you. Evidently she trusts you. Your being there could save us a lot of backing and filling."

"I'll be glad to help," Peter told him.

"I'm playing it straight with you, Styles. If you come across anything on your own, play it straight with me, huh?"

The main hall downstairs was dotted with little groups of people, all in earnest conversation. Tresh's weeding-out process was apparently well under way. The people here were the kitchen crew, the house servants, most of the people who'd not been involved with the morning's work on the terrace. Tresh had set up in the breakfast room and was questioning these people one by one.

As Peter passed one of the French doors opening out onto the terrace, he saw Mark Fleming sitting on the little stone parapet that ran around the edge of the terrace, staring broodingly down across the lawns toward the jumping course. On impulse, Peter went out to him.

Fleming turned as Peter approached. Black glasses hid his eyes. "Any news of Carol?" he asked urgently.

"Nothing. Still asleep as far as I know. Hours, the doctor said."

"The longer the better," Fleming said. "Going to be hell for her when they pounce on her."

"The County Attorney isn't a bad guy," Peter said. "He's asked me to be there when she's questioned."

"Is he so sure?"

"Sure?"

"That she's guilty! Else why a friend in court?"

"I don't think he's made up his mind."

"I keep telling myself she couldn't have done it," Fleming said. "And yet—"

"It's by no means a certainty," Peter said.

"You wouldn't kid me?"

"No." Peter hesitated. "You're genuinely fond of her?"

A bitter smile twisted Fleming's lips. "You been reading the papers, haven't you? Big sex wing-ding. This is a hell of a way to make a living, Styles. You can't have a bowel movement without somebody reporting on how you looked and what you were thinking about at the time. I sometimes think no money or fame or the worship of millions of people is worth the total lack of privacy." He kicked at the flagstones. "Yes, I'm genuinely fond of Carol. You want to interview me about it?"

"Not for publication," Peter said. "Carol's going to need friends. I'd like to find the real ones."

The eyes behind the black glasses studied Peter thoughtfully for a moment. "You haven't known Carol since she was a kid."

"Fourteen she was."

"Then you don't know the woman she is now, do you?"

"What I read in the papers."

"Bull," Fleming said. "Plain, unadulterated bull!"

"All right. What kind of person is she?"

"Everybody is something different to everybody," Fleming said. "There's a front you put up and what you are. Carol's front is for the public. Glamor. Sex. An open disregard of the moral standards of the housewife back home. Living her own life and to hell with what anyone thinks. Front. Nothing but front. The only difference between Carol and that housewife is that when she's being herself, she still has no privacy, and everyone interprets what she does in terms of the front. The real Carol is something else again."

Listening, Peter thought he knew the sound of real regard, real affection.

"It's rare in this day and age for any one person to go through life with just one other person," Fleming said. "If you read history, I guess it's always been rare. The housewife we were talking about probably had an affair or two in school or college. Maybe there was an interim between school and marriage and she had a couple more in that time. Then she gets married, and maybe she spends the rest of her life with that one husband. But along the way her foot slips here and there. I think that's an average pattern. People look at her and they think she's a one-man woman. That's supposed to be the norm.

"Carol was sixteen when she first came to Hollywood. At eighteen she was a name. She couldn't blow her nose without some jerk writing about it in the paper. She couldn't have a cup of coffee with a guy at a corner drugstore without notice being taken. If she did or didn't have an affair with someone, it was talked about as if she had. When she really got attached to someone and started to 'go steady,' the trumpets blew. The studio built the romance, the gossip girls built it. She didn't have the unobserved quiet of our housewife gal. She was pushed and pushed until she herself believed she was in love—and she married her first husband, a snotty-nosed juvenile, with spotlights focused on them. Without all the publicity she might have had a quiet thing with him, like our housewife, and passed on. That first marriage didn't work. An older man with professional grace and charm was number two. Because she'd been pushed into marriage number one, it had no real roots. More publicity. More hoopla. A divorce and a second marriage. Again our housewife would have moved through that one unnoticed. Not Carol. Nothing was unnoticed. Then came a real glamor boy, Douglas Teale. Leading man. Ladies' man. He played opposite her in a couple of pictures. She was on a merry-go-round now. Another divorce and another highly publicized marriage. Our housewife was just feeling her way at this stage of her life. Carol, in the bright glitter of stardom, was panicked by her life. She couldn't move without the professional keyhole peepers at her heels in full cry.

"When the marriage to Doug Teale was on the rocks, Garrity came along. Old, rich, safe. Panic took her to him, to the kind of protection he offered. And with the hounds baying at her heels, she married him. It was now a routine. Now she doesn't look like the housewife. The housewife was never pushed, so she never panicked. Carol's not independent and devil-may-care. She's frightened and insecure. She's not sophisticated. She's a little girl, only just beginning to grow up. Maybe she's still the kid you knew when she was fourteen. If she had a chance—any chance at all for privacy—I think she could find the right man if she wasn't driven by the Hollywood furies. I wish to God I could be that man." Fleming's voice was bitter. "Not that we'd have a chance. Not that we'd be let alone to work out a way of life."

"And there is Francis X. Garrity," Peter said when Fleming didn't go on.

Fleming laughed. It was a mirthless sound from deep inside him. "That joker!"

"I don't know whether Carol told you that she came to me for help," Peter said. "I never got a chance to hear from her why she needed help. But she did suggest Garrity might be at the root of her troubles."

"I know why she went to you," Fleming said. "We talked about it. I urged her to go. I couldn't help her. Garrity's little Gestapo was on my trail every minute. Anyhow, someone's gunning for me."

"Oh?"

"You've heard about the saddle girth incident?"

"So you know that was meant for you," Peter said.

"Of course I know. And if you were in my shoes, you wouldn't need three guesses at who was responsible."

"Garrity?"

"Who else? He's played it deadpan from the start, as though he thought it was aimed at Carol. But you notice he didn't call the cops. He's just waiting for another way to get at me. Well, I'm waiting for him to move!"

"Why didn't you report it to the police?"

"My dear idiot friend, do you know what would happen if I did? Four million more press releases about Carol and me. More dirt where there is no dirt. You finally reach a point in this business where you handle your own problems." The black glasses stared levelly at Peter. "You've already learned that lesson."

"Have I?"

Fleming's lips moved in a hard smile. "I checked in on you last night, Styles, on my way to bed. I thought you might have sobered up enough to discuss Carol's problem with me."

Peter felt the small hairs rising on the back of his neck.

"I saw what you saw when you looked in your mirror this morning," Fleming said.

"My room must have been like Grand Central Station!" Peter said, his voice shaken.

"You haven't made a noise about it," Fleming said, "nor has anyone else. So I take it I was your only visitor after the fact."

Peter's mouth felt dry. "You didn't try to wake me?"

"I got out of there fast," Fleming said. "I didn't want any part of it. I've been waiting for the big laugh, but it hasn't come."

"I saw the model for that clown face a little while ago in the library," Peter said.

"The Luks painting? I thought of that, too. Of course I didn't see poor old Rex."

"Duplicate," Peter said.

"Let me tell you something you may not know," Fleming said. He tossed his cigarette out on the lawn and watched the smoke curl up in the windless afternoon sunshine. "When Carol went to Hollywood twenty years ago, she was just a green kid—talented, but with no knowledge of the ropes. It's a highly competitive business. Cutthroat. Most people aren't very nice to you. If you're a woman, the other women fear you and hate you. You may take their jobs from them. The men look on you as a new piece of meat in town. The big shots may let you alone because of the caste system. It's not a good idea for a male star to be seen in public with extra girls. The jerks make their passes at you with promises, if you'll go to bed with them, that they'll get you next to some big director—like Monty Spain. Almost nobody is just plain, simply nice to you. It wasn't very different for Carol than anyone else. But she had a piece of luck. There was a fellow there in his mid-thirties—she was sixteen or seventeen, mind you. He was a competent bit player. He took Carol in tow, no ax to grind. He showed her the ropes. He got her to the good casting directors. He helped her break the ice. He just did it because he was a nice guy. He'd been a greenhorn once himself. He didn't make passes at her. He didn't have an affair with her. He was just a good friend. His name was Rex Barton."

Peter nodded slowly.

"So he winds up with a clown's face painted on him," Fleming said. "You were another good friend, even before Barton, Styles. And you wind up a clown. Coincidence, you think?"

Peter didn't answer.

"I could be next," Fleming said. "Carol's newest friend."

"You're still pointing at Garrity," Peter said.

"Who else? Oh, I know what his line must have been to you, Styles. Understanding husband. Deeply in love. Has to face the fact that Carol will have affairs. Waiting for the day she'll settle down quietly with him. All he wants to do is protect her from harm. Like that, wasn't it?"

"Could be a tape recording," Peter said dryly. "Let me ask you a question. You were rehearsing a scene with Carol on the terrace just before the lunch break. When I left, Garrity was there watching. Do you know if he left the terrace while you were rehearsing?"

Fleming laughed again. "Not likely. He watches us like a hawk."

"But can you say for certain that he didn't leave?"

Fleming frowned. "One of the ways I try to keep from exploding at him is to try to pretend he isn't there. I can't honestly say whether he was or wasn't. I'd blotted him out. Why do you ask?"

"Matter of alibi," Peter said.

"Show me how to make trouble for him and I'll be happy to testify that way," Fleming said.

"One thing you can do," Peter said. "Keep the business of what you saw in my room last night to yourself. I've already told it to the County Attorney, so I'm not hiding it from the police. But I have the feeling if it doesn't leak out, the person responsible won't be able to resist letting me know that he knows."

"As I wasn't able to resist," Fleming said.

"Something like that."

"I could have done it, you know," Fleming said. "I was there. I could have looked on you as a rival."

"Did you?"

"Look on you as a rival? Perhaps I did. Do! But I didn't paint your face, Styles. My mind doesn't work that indirectly."

Shortly after that the outside world began to invade the Black Glass City. The first news had gone out on radio and television just after noon. By three o'clock Marlingham began to swarm with the unwanted. The big front gates were chained off as they had been on Peter's arrival, with the regular gateman augmented by a State Trooper. An attempt was made to keep out the already eager sightseers, but legitimate representatives of the various news media were admitted. As for the sightseers, with several hundred acres of property boundaries unguarded and impossible to police, they simply avoided the gates and found dozens of other ways to reach the big house on the hill. The place crawled with cameras, hoping to get pictures of the famous movie people involved.

In addition to newsmen and sightseers there were others with varying rights to be there—agents representing some of the actors, an expensive-looking battery of legal talent, sweeping up to the front door in an air-conditioned Cadillac, representing the picture company; another lawyer representing the late Clarissa Moffet; neighbors, who in normal conditions would have offered help and sympathy, still came, though there was no one left to receive them for the Moffet family.

Monty Spain's camera crew literally stood guard over their expensive equipment. Souvenir hunters, trying to look as though they had a right to be there, seeped into the house itself.

Ben Jacobs found himself and his investigation inundated. Tempers flared. An emergency call went out to the trooper barracks for extra men. People who had a right to be there were pushed around by nervy troopers, and people with no right to be there were treated with courtesy. Stairways to the second floor were guarded carefully, lest snoopers get up into the murder room or the sickroom where Carol Richmond slept, watched by a policewoman inside and a trooper outside the door.

"Given the chance, the bastards would crash in and tear the nightgown off her to take home to their grandchildren," Jacobs said angrily to Peter. "What we need is the state militia."

After an hour or two, some sort of order was restored. Troopers, reinforced by Jim Walters' crew, set up a cordon at a distance of about a hundred yards from the house. Everybody who didn't belong was pushed back outside that line, and they roamed the grounds, hoping to get a view of someone important from a distant rise of ground.

The press camped in the house. The Monster, aware that the life of his picture teetered dangerously in the balance, set up a bar and provided sandwiches and other goodies in the big dining room. Ben Jacobs, in self-defense, had promised a statement as soon as he could get a free moment.

Among the official representatives of the fourth estate was Peter's friend, Bill Tompkins. *Newsview,* without hourly deadlines, had sent the man on their staff who knew most about the movie business.

"Devery assumes you consider yourself assigned to this story," Tompkins told Peter when he found him in the second-floor room which had been assigned to him with Carol occupying his original room.

"I may have a story to write when it's all over," Peter said grimly. "The shocking hunger of everyone for the gory details. This is a tragedy, not a public carnival."

"These people fight for publicity and public interest every day of their lives, Peter. Keeping the public interested in them is big business. They can't hope to turn off the faucet when the news is unpleasant. Their love affair with the public is for better or for worse."

"I know," Peter said angrily. "I caught some little bastard trying to snitch a priceless Japanese print off the wall in the front hall. This was home to a gracious woman who loved the place and cherished its dignity. Suddenly it's crawling with maggots."

"It was a jolt to me when the news came through," Bill Tompkins said. "I told you, I liked the old girl. Did you get a chance to meet her at all?"

"Briefly. She wanted me to help preserve the Marlingham image. God help her, this is all that will be remembered. Her own slaughter!"

"Can we stop skating around the edge of the pond,

Peter? Is Carol guilty? The rest of us ordinary mortals have had no official statement, but it seems open and shut."

"I don't really have any right to talk to you, Bill. I'm a key witness. I'm also Carol's friend."

"Is there any chance she didn't do it?"

"She hasn't made any statement yet."

"But you think—?"

"I think she's going to say that she didn't," Peter said. "All the evidence they've found so far points the other way. But Jacobs, the prosecutor, is a decent guy. He's also a pro. He knows there are a few loopholes. He may not lower the boom until he's got those loopholes plugged up. But if he can't plug them, he's still got enough to bring a first-degree murder charge."

A few minutes later Jacobs justified Peter's estimate of him. He sent word he would meet with the press in the dining room. Peter and Bill were notified and they went down to the crowded room to hear what Jacobs had to say.

The sandy-haired prosecutor looked tired to Peter, as though his nerves were badly frazzled. But he managed to present a patient, good-humored front to reporters and photographers.

"We have no official statement to make yet," he said. "You must all know that we haven't been able to question Carol Richmond. We don't know what her story is or will be. She was seen by two witnesses in the murder room, holding the murder weapon in her hand, spattered with the victim's blood. There are no other fingerprints but hers on the candlestick which was the murder weapon."

"So what else is there?" someone asked.

"The time elements in the case aren't easy to nail down," Jacobs said. "Carol Richmond and her husband came up from the terrace outside there after a rehearsal. They had a conversation in the sitting room of their suite. Mr. Garrity left to hold a conversation with Peter Styles. Half an hour later he went back to his suite and found his wife in the bedroom, standing over the murdered woman. He called for help and Styles joined him. That's that. What we don't know, until we can talk to Miss Richmond, is this. If she killed Mrs. Moffet, that's that. But if she says she didn't—"

"Naturally she'll say that!"

"She may," Jacobs said. "If she does, then we're faced with the possibility that sometime after her husband left her to go talk to Styles, she went into the bedroom and found Mrs. Moffet there, dead. It would have been a shocking sight. Miss Richmond may have tried to help the dead woman, accounting for the blood stains on her. She could, thoughtlessly, have picked up the candlestick. I said the time elements were hard to nail down. The medical examiner can't narrow the time of death down to anything so exact as fifteen or twenty minutes. What I'm saying is that we can't say for certain that Mrs. Moffet wasn't killed before Miss Richmond and her husband came up to the room. It's not impossible, and there's no way we can prove from medical testimony that it isn't so."

"You got any other suspects?"

"We've spent so much of the last couple of hours trying to keep this house from being torn apart, brick by brick, that our investigation hasn't moved very far. But if I had another suspect, I wouldn't tell you. I can't keep you from the obvious, but we'll have no statements about anyone until we make an arrest. There'll be no arrest until Miss Richmond is in shape to be questioned."

"When will that be?"

"I'm not a doctor," Jacobs said. "Maybe soon. Maybe later tonight. Maybe tomorrow."

"Why did she do it?"

Jacobs ran a hand across his face. “Until I question Miss Richmond—” He spread his hands.

“People in the area are pretty sore about this, Mr. Jacobs. Mrs. Moffet was well liked.”

“Not so sore they won’t try to tear the buttons off the actors’ clothes for souvenirs if they get the chance,” Jacobs said sharply. “That’s all, ladies and gentlemen. We haven’t made an arrest and we probably won’t until Miss Richmond has been questioned. There seems to be an obvious answer, but we haven’t wrapped it up and we can’t until after that questioning. I make you one suggestion. Don’t hang anyone in print until you know who’s guilty.”

3

BUCK MARSHALL, wearing his white houseman's coat, the inevitable black glasses, and with a cigarette dangling out of the corner of his mouth, was waiting outside the dining room when the press conference broke up. He was waiting for Peter, and made it known by calling out to him over the heads of the crowd.

"Hey, Pete!"

Peter waited for the crowd to move toward The Monster's improvised bar. "I take it that means me," he said.

"Francis X. wants a little yakety with you," Buck said.

"Where is he?"

"Like you, they moved him," Buck said. "Other end of the hall on the second floor. Incidentally, I persuaded the gendarmes to let me take your stuff into your new room. You're all moved."

"Thanks."

"I got a look at Carol," he said. "White like a ghost." He smiled his crooked little smile. "Historic moment. She was alone in bed."

"You haven't got my favorite sense of humor, Buck," Peter said.

"Excuse it," Buck said, still grinning. "Free association, I guess you'd call it. Bed—Carol—get it?"

"I get it, chum."

"We're gonna have rough days ahead," Buck said. "Francis is gonna miss her real bad. He's goofy in love with her, you know."

"Miss her?"

"They don't just spank your behind and send you home with a good talking-to for murder."

"You've made up your mind?"

"What's to make up?" Buck said, looking genuinely surprised.

"I'd like to hear your life story sometime, Buck," Peter said. "You're a puzzle, you know?"

"Not a very interesting story," Buck said. "Come on, I'll take you to Francis." They started for the stairs. "I was working in a health club in New York. Locker boy. Francis was one of the customers. Somebody told him he should work out every day to keep his pot down. He was a free tipper, so I figured out things to do for him." Buck gave Peter a sly side glance. "Golden Boy I used to call him. He was kind of lonely, I guess. Talk to anyone who'd listen to him. I listened. It came up the jackpot for me. He hired me to work for him, personal. That was fifteen years ago. I was like one of the family, like I told you. Ate my meals with him, went to the movies with him, and to the ball games. That's all he liked: movies and ball games. He bought me clothes—the best of everything. I actually got to like him!" Buck chuckled. "Then, about four years ago, he got the Carol bug. So off to Hollywood we go. Next thing I knew, they're married. I figured that was the end for me, but no. I didn't eat with them, but everything else was the same. For a while I thought I might take over his bedroom duties, but Carol gave me the brush. I guess she thought it was too risky to play around with someone under the same roof."

"That was her reason, you think?" Peter said, half angry, half amused.

"What else? I'm a strong, healthy guy. Francis ain't exactly much of a lover any more—if he ever was. It would have been a pleasure, but she wasn't having any. Well, I guess when the law gets through with her, we'll be heading back to New York, Francis and me, and a season box at Yankee Stadium. I won't mind. I admit it makes you restless to be around a dame like Carol and you can't lay a finger on her."

"I can imagine. This it?" They'd come to a door at the end of the hall.

"Yeah," Buck said. He lowered his voice. "Be nice, huh, Pete? The old boy needs friends." Without knocking, Buck opened the door and went in, beckoning to Peter to follow him.

Francis X. Garrity was sitting in an armchair by the window. The late-afternoon sun was casting long shadows across the lawn outside. Garrity turned his head, and the owlish glasses focused on Peter. Peter was shocked by his appearance. His eyes were red-rimmed; his cheeks looked sunken in like a sick man; his skin was sallow and unhealthy.

"Thanks for bringing him, Buck," he said, his voice weak.

"My pleasure, boss," Buck said. "Holler if you need anything. I'll be next door. They gave me the room next to you."

"That's fine, boy," Garrity said. "Sit down, Mr. Styles—if you can spare me a moment."

Buck Marshall left them.

"There's no one here I can talk to, Styles," Garrity said. "These people aren't my friends, you know. Oh, they treat me nicely because Carol is a big star. But Carol's in trouble now, and so to them I'm nobody."

"It's every man for himself when there's trouble," Peter said.

"I've been trying to get legal help," Garrity said. "I suppose the best criminal lawyer in the east is J. C. Kramer. I've been in touch with his office. Kramer's in court with a case. He's sending an assistant up to talk to me. Carol will need the best."

"You can't do better than Kramer," Peter said.

"I'm worried by the advice he gave me," Garrity said. "Carol's not to make any sort of statement until Kramer's man gets here. How can I get to her to tell her that? They won't let me in her room. Carol's not someone to be silent about her troubles. If they ask her questions, she'll answer."

"Let's face it," Peter said. "If Carol's guilty, not talking isn't going to help her very much. If Kramer knew the details, he'd probably agree. The evidence is pretty overwhelming. If she's innocent and denies her guilt, that's the best thing she could do. Let's look at the blackest side, Garrity. If Carol killed Mrs. Moffet, her only possible defense will be temporary insanity. It won't matter much what she says now if that's to be her defense. It becomes a matter for psychiatrists then."

"You think that's it, don't you?"

"If Carol killed her. There's no sane reason for her attacking a woman she scarcely knew. Or is there?"

"Of course not."

"I keep going over other possibilities in my mind," Peter said quietly. "If Carol's innocent, and I choose to assume that for the moment—"

"Bless you!" Garrity said unexpectedly.

"If she's innocent, then Mrs. Moffet was killed in your room before you and Carol came up from the terrace. Most of the working company was on the terrace till the lunch break. You were there."

"For all but a few minutes," Garrity said.

Peter sat very still.

"I came into the house for the mail," Garrity said. "It's brought from the post office a little after eleven and placed on the big table in the entrance hall. I was expecting some business correspondence, and I went in about ten past eleven. I remember looking at my watch."

"Anybody see you in the house?"

"Sherry Garth was at the table in the hall getting her mail," Garrity said, his wide eyes fixed on Peter.

Tresh had been questioning people for alibis, Peter knew. It was probably no secret what he was checking out. Garrity could easily know that. Had he let this drop so that it would seem completely casual before the questioning came around to him? Or was it as innocent as it sounded? This wasn't, Peter thought, the moment to press it. It struck him as he sat there looking at the shriveled Garrity, that the one thing that had been missing from the very beginning was the smallest hint of motive for the murder—motive for Carol or anyone else. Mrs. Moffet had irritated some of these people by her possessive attitude toward the big house, but you don't kill an old woman for that.

It was the first question Ben Jacobs was to ask Carol Richmond in a very little while. "*Why did you kill Mrs. Moffet?*"

The "why" was the missing link. Carol had had the opportunity, and so, it appeared, had Garrity, and several others who were in the house. Peter had been in the house himself, and Sherry Garth, and Orrin Pell, and a whole staff of servants.

But *why?*

Twilight fell over Marlingham.

It was martini time.

The whole population of the Black Glass City, augmented by newsmen and newswomen, lawyers, agents, waited. They waited for what would almost certainly be the end of suspense for them: the questioning of Carol Richmond, her arrest, and the probable end of Montague Spain's epic. While they waited, they were suspended in space. None of them, reasonably enough, felt any personal loss as a result of Clarissa Moffet's death. There were feelings about Carol, but with the possible exceptions of Peter, Mark Fleming, and Francis X. Garrity there was no real anxiety for her. She was a big star, the bright ornament on top of a gilded Christmas tree. She was alone. She might cost them jobs. She might cost the clients of some of the legal talent a hatful of money. Most of them felt only the need to get on with things—get on with the picture or get on with their packing and go home.

There was excitement in the air, but little grief or concern.

Monty Spain's bartenders and waiters began to work at high speed. Voices became a little louder. Laughter became a little shriller. In a far corner of the dining room where the bar was set up, Monty Spain sat in his custom-built armchair, surrounded by Louis Beaujon, Ron Samuels, and one of his cameramen. He was drinking a tall glass of milk, his little pig eyes darting around the room. There was just a chance that the sleeping woman upstairs might be innocent. If she was, somewhere in this room, somewhere in this crowd that was beginning to sound and act like a shrill celebration, there must be someone else who had beaten Clarissa Moffet to death. You could almost feel The Monster willing that to be so, willing the guilty person to reveal himself. In the babel of sound, in the haze of tobacco smoke, in the atmosphere of forced gaiety, the faces seemed false, masked, self-protective.

In a room upstairs Dr. Graham sat beside Carol Richmond's bed. She was propped up against some pillows, her dark violet eyes wide open, their pupils enlarged by drugs or fear. Methodically Dr. Graham had gone through the blood pressure routines and he was just putting his stethoscope away in his bag. He looked at Carol with something like distaste.

"You must know, Miss Richmond, that the County Attorney is waiting anxiously to talk to you. It's my duty to tell him when you're able to stand up under questioning. I can tell him now that, physically, there's no reason why he shouldn't see you."

"You sound, Doctor, as though they questioned you in these parts with whips!" Carol's voice was clear, a little high, a little tense.

"If you find me unsympathetic, Miss Richmond, it's because Mrs. Moffet was a great and good friend of mine."

"And I am not," Carol said. "Fair enough. But as a doctor, surely you must have some concern for my mental stability."

"That's for the court psychiatrists," Graham said coldly.

"My dear idiot doctor," Carol said. "I'm talking about this moment. I'm not going to be stared at by prosecutors and policemen looking the way I must. There is a negligee in my room, and a brush and comb and makeup. Please have someone get them."

The policewoman who had been sitting on a chair in the corner of the room came over to the bed. "I'm Mrs. Howard," she said. "I'm afraid nothing can be touched in your room, Mrs. Garrity."

"You'll be good enough to call me 'Miss Richmond,' "

Carol said. "Not even my purse with my lipstick and compact in it?"

"I'm afraid not."

"I see. In that case there is a Mr. Zachary, who is head of the makeup department. Perhaps you'd be good enough to ask him for the loan of a comb and brush and makeup. He'll know what I need."

"I'll see what I can do," the policewoman said.

Mrs. Howard went over to the door, opened it, and spoke to the trooper stationed outside. The doctor, looking uncomfortable, spoke again.

"I'll tell Ben Jacobs you can see him," he said.

"Give me time to get ready for him, Doctor."

"My duty is to report to him at once," the doctor said.

"So you won't even wish me luck," Carol said, and she gave him a bitter little smile.

A cool one, the doctor thought. He looked at her with frank hostility. These people lived their whole lives without regard for anyone else, he told himself. Flaunt their love affairs. And now, in an outbreak of uncontrolled temper, a fine, good woman had been senselessly exterminated. No, he didn't wish this gaudy woman luck. Let her pay for it in spades. If he was asked, officially, he could say with all honesty he saw no signs of mental disturbance. In fact he said just that five minutes later to Ben Jacobs, whom he found pacing the library.

"She's ready then?" Jacobs said.

"Came out of it like a baby waking up," Dr. Graham said. "Reasonably normal pulse, normal blood pressure. Full of little jokes. Demanding her lipstick!"

Jacobs grinned at the indignant young doctor. "A woman without her lipstick is a little like a man without his pants," he said. He beckoned to the stenotype operator. "Let's go," he said. "I want Sergeant Tresh in on this."

A few minutes later Jacobs, Tresh, and the stenotype operator entered Carol's room. The emergency supplies from Mr. Zachary had evidently arrived. Carol sat in her bed, amost erect, looking alert and, Jacobs thought, unquestionably very lovely.

"Dr. Graham tells me you're ready to talk to us, Mrs. Garrity," Jacobs said. "I'm Ben Jacobs, the County Attorney."

"Please be good enough to call me Miss Richmond," Carol said.

"As you please. What you say will be taken down by my stenotype operator, Miss Richmond, and you understand it can be used against you."

"I'm not entitled to have anyone here to represent me?"

"No. Not yet."

"I'm under arrest?"

"Yes. At the moment you're being held as a material witness."

"I'm not charged with murder?"

So very cool, Jacobs thought. "Not yet, Miss Richmond."

"I'd like Peter Styles here," Carol said.

"I'm afraid that's not possible," Jacobs said.

"I would be much more co-operative, Mr. Jacobs."

"How clearly do you understand the position you're in, Miss Richmond?" Jacobs asked.

"I am apparently going to be charged with killing a woman I scarcely knew," Carol said. "I had spoken to her perhaps a half dozen times. I had said important things to her like 'Good morning' and 'Thank you for the flowers.' "

"You were found standing over her with the murder weapon in your hand," Jacobs said, his voice harsh, "your face and hands and clothing spattered with her blood."

A little shudder seemed to run over Carol's body, but she

held her head high and there was no sign of flinching in her eyes.

"Why did you kill Mrs. Moffet?" Jacobs demanded.

There was a moment of electric silence, and then Carol said: "I'd like Peter Styles here."

"My dear Miss Richmond—"

"My dear Mr. Jacobs," Carol cut in, her voice high-pitched but controlled, "my life is at stake. Everything I say is being ticked off on that machine. You're surrounding me like a pack of wolves. You expect me to let you tear me to pieces without anybody on my side—to help. God knows I need help, Mr. Jacobs. You've got that machine to record everything I say. I want a friend to hear what I say." She gave him a frozen smile. "I'm going to have Peter Styles here, Mr. Jacobs, or I'll take the Fifth Amendment or whatever it is."

"What about your husband?"

"I want Peter," she said quietly. "I trust him, and in the end he can speak for me publicly if it's necessary."

"It's not according to Hoyle, Miss Richmond."

"It's my life, Mr. Jacobs."

Jacobs had half expected this request, but not from so controlled a witness. He had imagined he might need Peter to calm Carol down, to get her into a state where she could talk at all.

Laughter from the floor below drifted upstairs. What should have been a wake for Clarissa Moffet was turning into a high-pitched drunken party. Jacobs wanted to move and move fast. He could hear the higher-ups demanding to know why he had delayed so long in making an arrest. If Peter's presence would expedite things, why not? He sent Tresh to find Peter.

The wait was like something out of a dream—the beautiful woman sitting up in bed, a Cheshire-cat smile on her bright scarlet lips. She'd won the first round.

And "Do you have a cigarette, Mr. Jacobs?" And "Thank you," as he held his lighter for her. Like a drawing-room comedy, not a moment of truth. And an unanswered question hanging in space.

"You knew Mrs. Moffet, Mr. Jacobs?" Carol asked.

"Very well."

"She loved this place. I think she hated us for putting it to our particular uses. But she needed the money, didn't she?"

"I suppose she did. Like a lot of people in this area, I was indebted to her," Jacobs said. "She helped put me through college and law school."

"That doesn't disqualify you as a prosecutor, Mr. Jacobs?"

"Why should it?"

"You couldn't be called impartial, could you?"

"I'm not required to be impartial, Miss Richmond. It's my job to arrest the killer, prosecute successfully, and send him to the gas chamber."

" 'Him,' Mr. Jacobs?"

"Figure of speech, I'm afraid."

The almost mysterious smile widened. "Don't be afraid, Mr. Jacobs."

Jacobs prayed silently for Peter's quick arrival. He understood something of the magic that had made this woman a star. In spite of himself he found himself drawn to her. He forced himself to remember the scene in the bedroom down the hall where he'd viewed the remains of Clarissa Moffet.

And then Tresh came back with Peter.

Peter was frankly astonished at what he saw. The shocked, blank face he'd last seen was gone. Carol was herself, it seemed. A little pale, a little overstimulated, but herself.

"Thanks for coming, darling," she said.

"You're feeling better?" A banality. What else?

"The quiet before Mr. Jacobs' storm," she said. "He's been very nice so far, Peter, but I don't think it's going to last."

"You understand, Styles, that what goes on here is privileged," Jacobs said. "It will be on the record. What you say will also be on the record."

"I understand."

"I asked you a question, Miss Richmond, before we stopped to send for Mr. Styles," Jacobs said. He gave a little signal to the stenotype operator. "Why did you kill Mrs. Moffet?"

Peter was standing by the bed, and Carol reached out and her cool fingers closed tightly over his hand. "I can't answer that question, Mr. Jacobs," she said steadily. "I can't tell you why I killed her, because I didn't kill her."

The stenotype machine made a faint clicking noise. Jacobs, Tresh, and the policewoman stared at Carol. Peter could feel her fingers tighten on his hand. Here we go, he thought, with some kind of story.

"You were found standing over her with a bloody candlestick in your hand," Jacobs said.

"I've lived my whole life with that kind of evidence hanging over my head, Mr. Jacobs," Carol said. "If I'm seen with a man, I'm supposed to have been in bed with him. It doesn't follow, you understand, but it's always assumed. I may have been standing over Mrs. Moffet with a candlestick in my hand, but I didn't kill her."

"*May* have been?" Jacobs said. "Your husband saw you; Mr. Styles saw you."

"It's not an easy story to tell, because I can't tell it all," Carol said.

"Can't or won't?"

"Can't, Mr. Jacobs. That's the worst of it. For quite a long time I've been awake, but I didn't let the doctor or Mrs. Howard know because I've been trying to remember. *Trying so damned hard!*"

Jacobs glanced at Peter. He'd been afraid of something like this. The everything-went-black department. "Tell us what you do remember, Miss Richmond."

Her bright red lips trembled slightly. "I had been rehearsing a scene on the terrace," she said. "When Monty called a break for lunch, my husband and I went upstairs to our suite. I had sent a note to Peter telling him I wanted to see him—that I'd come to his room to talk to him when the rehearsal ended. I asked Francis to run an errand for me, and then—then he told me he'd intercepted the note. Even my own personal maid was part of the spy system he has watching me. Francis insisted on talking to Peter himself. So he went down the hall to Peter's room." Carol drew a deep breath. "It—it was sort of the straw that broke the camel's back. I was furious. I went out of the room and downstairs, looking for Monty."

"Montague Spain," Jacobs said, glancing at the stenotype man. "Why did you want to see him?"

"To tell him I couldn't go on with the picture with Francis here peering over my shoulder. If anyone could get Francis away from here, Monty could. If anything interferes with a picture of his, he can move mountains."

"And did you see him, talk to him?"

"No. He was involved with a long-distance call to the Coast. I knew that could take half an hour or so. I went back up to the suite fuming. Francis was still with Peter. The bathroom adjoins the bedroom. I decided to freshen up for lunch. So—so I went into the bedroom." A long, shuddering sigh escaped Carol. "She was there—there on the bed. The room started to go round and round. I knew she must be dead—or dying. My impulse was to help. I went to her—touched her. When I took my hand away, it was red with her blood. And then—that's all I remember until I came to, stretched out on the bed in Peter's room, with the doctor and Peter and Francis there."

"You don't remember your husband coming into the room and seeing you?"

"No." She was suddenly almost inaudible.

"You don't remember Styles coming, carrying you to his room?"

"No."

"When did you pick up the candlestick?"

"I—I don't know."

"Where was it when you came into the room?"

"Believe me, Mr. Jacobs, I don't remember it—or seeing it, or touching it."

"You did handle it, Miss Richmond. Yours are the only fingerprints on it."

"If Peter says I handled it, then I handled it." She looked up at Peter, a strained look in the violet eyes.

"You had it in your hand when I first saw you, Carol," Peter said.

"There was blood on your clothes, Miss Richmond, and on your glasses. How do you account for that?"

"I can't even try to account for it. I must have tried to help her. The blood was on my hands—I may have touched my clothes, the glasses."

"You can't remember anything after the first moment in the bedroom," Jacobs said, "but you remember quite clearly going up to the suite with your husband, your argument with him, his leaving to find Styles, your going downstairs to find Mr. Spain, and then returning upstairs to your suite again. All that's perfectly clear?"

"Perfectly."

"Did anyone see you downstairs on that trip to find Spain? How did you know he was talking long-distance to the coast?"

"Ron Samuels came out of Monty's office just as I got there. Ron is the public relations man for the company. He told me Monty was on the phone."

That could be checked out, Peter knew. It would cut down the amount of time Carol could have spent in the bedroom by quite a bit. She couldn't have killed Clarissa Moffet before she went downstairs. She couldn't have gone wandering through the house like a bloodstained Lady Macbeth.

"You have nothing to add to what took place in the bedroom?" Jacobs asked.

"Nothing. I remember seeing her. I remember going to her. Then I was in a kind of swirling fog. I came to in Peter's room. That's absolutely all, Mr. Jacobs."

Jacobs lit a cigarette, his face pale and tense. It could be true, he told himself. The gory spectacle on the bed could have driven a less high-strung person than Carol Richmond into shock. The trip downstairs, a conversation with Samuels, used up time. She could still have done it on her return, but it tightened the time schedule.

"There are other things we need to know that I'm sure you can remember, Miss Richmond," Jacobs said.

"Please ask me," Carol said.

"Do you have any explanation of what Mrs. Moffet might have been doing in your rooms?"

"No. When we first came, she used to bring flowers."

"She had a basket of flowers when she went into the house this morning," Peter said.

"There were no flowers in the room," Jacobs said. "What else could have taken her there? Had you sent for her to make some complaint or ask for something special?"

"No. As a matter of fact, I hadn't seen her to talk to for several days."

"Your husband?"

Carol's lips tightened. "You'll have to ask him," she said.

"Then you can give us no explanation of why she should have been in your suite—in your bedroom?"

"None."

"All right, Miss Richmond, let's go back further than that. Two days ago you went to New York. You went to see Styles. You told him you were in trouble; that someone was trying to destroy you as an actress and a person. You never got to tell him what it was all about because your husband arrived on the scene. But you did tell him you thought your husband might be your enemy. Please explain that."

She closed her eyes for a moment. "Has anyone told you about the things that have happened to me?"

"Your husband told Styles," Jacobs said.

"Someone even tried to kill me by cutting my saddle girth," she said.

Jacobs hesitated. "There's some question about that, Miss Richmond. We understand you shifted saddles with Mr. Fleming before you started out on your ride. It was the girth on Mr. Fleming's saddle, not yours, that was cut."

Her eyes were suddenly wide open. "Oh, my God!" she whispered.

"What made you think your husband might be your enemy?"

She turned her face to one side, her eyes averted from Peter and Jacobs. "More than ever, if what you say is true," she said. "Oh, my God!"

"Please tell us, Miss Richmond."

She was still clinging to Peter, and her bright red fingernails bit into the palm of his hand. "I suppose, in a way, I'm responsible," she said. "I should never have married Francis. It was miserably unfair to him. He seemed so calm, so secure, to ask for so little. He offered a kind of safety I'd never had. I should have known he couldn't give what he promised or ask for as little as he thought he could. It was his dream that sooner or later I would come to the end of my career as an actress and settle down to being his wife. I told him I could be an actress as long as I could walk in front of a camera—even if I was playing grandmothers. He was sure, so sure, that I'd see it another way when my days as a big star were past. I was running, hiding—so I took what he offered. It wasn't fair."

"He was not your enemy then."

"No."

"But he became your enemy?"

"He couldn't do what he thought he could do. He wanted more than he thought he wanted. He became jealous of my work, jealous of my time, jealous of my associations with other people. He believed the kind of things that appear in print. Would you believe me if I told you that I've been married to Francis for nearly four years and that I've never been unfaithful to him—physically?"

Jacobs didn't answer.

"I see you read the papers," she said bitterly. "Oh, I've been attracted to other people. I may even be in love with someone else at the moment. I said physically faithful. I have been. But of course Francis doesn't believe that; wouldn't believe it if I swore the most sacred kind of oath. So to all intents and purposes I am, in Francis' book, an unfaithful wife in a highly unsuccessful marriage. And this has driven him off his own steady path. He has accused me of God knows what. The men I have known, the men I know now, are all clowns. I am a—"

"How's that?" Jacobs interrupted sharply. "The men you know are all clowns?"

"His phrase," Carol said.

"Go on," Jacobs said, in an odd voice.

"He was determined somehow to get me out of the business, to get me away somewhere, to get me to himself. He had me watched—by my own servants, by private detectives, by God knows who else. When things began to happen to me here—a stolen makeup kit, phony phone calls, a fake telegram, my invaluable script torn to shreds, and then what I thought was an actual attempt on my life—I could only wonder if it must not be Francis. Now you tell me the riding accident was aimed at Mark. Don't you see, Mark is the hobgoblin in Francis' life?"

"What could he have hoped to accomplish with the other things—the theft, the destruction of the script, the phone calls?" Jacobs asked.

"Working with a man like Monty Spain is a high-pressure business, Mr. Jacobs. You need all your energy, all your concentration. If you're distracted, made anxious, you begin to louse things up. Then Monty blows. Suddenly you're not functioning, you're driven to excesses of temperament and temper. You could crack up. The history of Hollywood is filled with stories of people who have gone to pieces under pressure—even suicides. People at the top of the heap like me!"

"Why would your husband want this?"

"Because if I went to pieces, he would have me to himself."

Jacobs lit a fresh cigarette. "Do you have a single scrap of evidence to prove that Garrity is responsible for any one of the things that happened to you?"

"No," she said promptly. "But who else?"

Jacobs glanced at Tresh with a silent question. The

Sergeant had nothing to add.

"May I ask Carol a question?" Peter asked.

Jacobs nodded.

"Rex Barton was an old friend of yours, wasn't he, Carol?"

"Poor Rex," she said. "He needed the job so badly. He lied about his riding and he was trying so hard to be ready for the moment when he'd have to show Monty."

"Tell us about your relationship with him."

"When I first went to Hollywood, I didn't know anyone. I didn't know the ropes. No one was very helpful. I—I was an attractive kid, and the wolves were all after me. The only person willing to help was Rex. He really got me started. There was never anything between us but friendship. I've always been grateful to him. Whenever I could, in the past, I've gotten him jobs in my pictures. That's all."

"Did your husband think there'd been more than that?"

"Everyone I ever look at or speak to has been in bed with me in Francis' book. Even you, Peter."

"Clowns," Peter said.

"You say that's what your husband called the men he imagined were your lovers, Miss Richmond?" Jacobs asked.

"I think I should tell you, Carol," Peter said, "that last night, while I was out cold from a drugged drink, someone painted a clown's face on me."

"Peter!"

"And I think I should tell you, Jacobs," Peter said, "that Francis Garrity told me that he did leave the terrace during this morning's rehearsal. He went into the house to get his mail. Sherry Garth was in the hall, he says, when he picked up his letters there."

Jacobs showed angry indecision. He turned and ground out his cigarette in an ash tray on a side table. "I have enough evidence to hold you, Miss Richmond, in spite of your story," he said. "But I'm not making a formal charge. Not yet. I urge you to try to remember more than you have."

"It's no use," she said. For the first time her controlled surface seemed to crack. She turned her head from side to side on the pillows. "This whole thing revolves around me, doesn't it? First Mark, then Rex, then Peter. Peter, please, please look out for yourself. And look out for Mark! He won't stop now that he's got a taste of it."

"Who won't stop, Miss Richmond?" Jacobs asked.

"Francis! Don't you see how it must be? He's gone out of his head about the men he thinks I'm interested in."

"And where does Mrs. Moffet fit into that pattern, Miss Richmond?"

"God only knows. Perhaps she knew something, saw something."

"And perhaps you killed her in that blank period of time you can't remember," Jacobs said.

"No!"

"You were under pressure. You said so yourself, Miss Richmond. You found Mrs. Moffet going through your private belongings. You went into an unreasoning anger and attacked her. You told us the history of Hollywood is filled with stories of crack-ups."

"No!" Carol cried out.

Jacobs' mouth was a hard, straight line. "Francis Garrity's fingerprints are not on that candlestick, Miss Richmond. You're full of theories about him, but you haven't presented one incriminating fact."

"His jealousy is a fact!"

And, Peter told himself, Garrity had easy access to the missing makeup kit, the torn-up script. He could have made the phone calls. He knew about the favorite uncle. He had brushed off the saddle girth incident, advising Jim Walters not to go to the police. He wandered freely about the grounds when the others were working. He could have reached Rex Barton before anyone else. He could easily have gone to Peter's room sometime during the previous evening and done that job. Not facts. But here, at least, were motive and opportunity.

The stubborn, angry look on Jacobs' face suggested he was thinking along the same lines and wasn't happy about it His easy case might not be as easy as it had looked.

4

THE TEMPO of the evening downstairs had developed into a kind of harsh gaiety. There had been no formal dinner. With the influx of outsiders, a buffet had been served, and through it all the martini pace had increased. A hi-fi system in one corner of the room had begun the evening by delivering soft dinner music, a regular part of the evening program. Now it blared jazz rhythms. It might have been expected that people would break up into small groups, or disappear to their rooms to wait. It didn't happen that way. The word had passed swiftly when Jacobs, Tresh, and Peter had gone to Carol's room. She would be talking now. Jobs were at stake. Futures were at stake. It was as if they all felt it would be safer to face whatever was to come together.

Some of the outsiders were noisily, obviously drunk. So much free liquor, poured out in unmeasured drinks, had taken its toll. Loud laughter seemed garishly out of place, yet defiant.

There were two noticeable absentees. Montague Spain had left the party early to go to his office. A hot telephone line from the Coast kept him busy. Anxious studio executives saw millions of dollars going down the drain. The

Monster was their only contact, their only hope.

Francis X. Garrity was the other missing member of the community. His absence was noted, but considered normal under the circumstances.

Word would come soon from upstairs, they all felt. Carol would be arrested, charged with murder, taken away—or the door would be left open as a result of some hoped-for loophole.

The aristocracy of the cast sat at a small table in a far corner of the noisy room—Mark Fleming, Sherry Garth, and Orrin Pell. Pell was darkly, sardonically drunk. Fleming seemed worn, tired, tense. His eyes kept darting toward the main door, expecting a messenger of doom to appear. Sherry Garth, eyes hidden by black glasses, chewed nervously on her lower lip.

"I'll bet no other Moffet ever lay dead in this house to the accompaniment of a Louis Armstrong trumpet," Pell said sourly. "Not a wet eye in the house."

"Nobody really knew her, Orrin," Sherry said, her voice on edge.

"I daresay in the slave quarters they weep for her," Pell said.

"What slave quarters?"

"The stables, the toolsheds. The men who cut the grass here thought highly of her."

"And the prosecutor, and the cops," Fleming said, his eyes on the door. "Thank God, Styles is up there or a little Chinese torture might be in order."

"Oh, you're wrong, old boy," Pell said with a wry smile. "Ideally Carol should be alone with the prosecutor. Country boy succumbs to the weaknesses of the flesh."

"Don't be nasty, Orrin," Sherry said.

Fleming's eyes narrowed, but he kept looking at the door.

"I'm being factual, my sweet," Pell said. "Left to her own

devices, our Carol would find a way out."

"Shut up, Orrin!" Fleming said sharply.

"Our tender-minded he-man," Pell said. "Come off it, Mark. There isn't a soul here who's thinking of anything but his own hide. We want Carol cleared because a year's work lies ahead of us if she is. That goes for the whole company. The newspaper boys want her arrested. Where's their story if the D.A. announces Mrs. Moffet was killed by an indignant houseman or stableboy? But Carol—poor Carol—only you are playing the melancholy role, Mark. I find it symbolically interesting that she's being questioned in bed."

Slowly, almost reluctantly, Fleming took his eyes away from the door. "I've had about enough from you, Orrin."

Pell reached for his highball glass on the table and drained it. He waved to one of the houseboys who came over and took the glass away for a refill. "What are the clichés?" he asked no one in particular. "Make your own bed and lie in it? Chickens home to roost? What do you suppose the old lady did that sent Carol into such a rage? Our Carol had few if any secrets. Open-book Carol."

A muscle rippled along Fleming's jaw, but his eyes were back at the door again. The word must come soon.

"Carol's reputation has been built by people like you, Orrin," Sherry Garth said. "You've never let her alone since your time of being close to her went by. Can't you bear the thought that anyone's regard for you should be temporary?"

"All is temporary, my sweet. All that matters is the present. This moment, this present, is one of suspense. Do we work tomorrow, or do we go job hunting? That's really all that concerns us."

The room was hot and full of smoke. One of the newsmen and a script girl were doing a fancy dance twist in the center of the floor to a hot Al Hirt tune. Ron Samuels was ogling a lady photographer at the bar. The rest of the room seemed to be milling about without any particular design. From time to time someone went to the door to look out into the corridor. To the people in this room it seemed that Jacobs was taking a long time to make up his mind about Carol. Newsmen and photographers were afraid they might try to slip Carol away from Marlingham with no chance for pictures or an interview.

"As for Carol's reputation," Pell said, sampling his fresh drink, "it was not made by me, sweetie, or anyone else but dear Carol herself. The old-time stars kept their carousing private, but not today. It was Liz and Dickie one year. It's Carol and Mark another year. How many crime reporters do you see in this room? Hell, most of the newspapers have sent their movie columnists and maybe a sports reporter or two. The Roman holiday is in fashion again. Our boys die in Viet Nam; the Red Chinese develop their own atomic bomb; but tomorrow's headlines will be: 'Carol Brains Society Matron.' "

"I've had just about enough, Orrin," Fleming said, his dark eyes smoldering.

"Wisest words you ever spoke," Pell said. "Just a small touch of Carol is enough for anyone. Old Rex Barton befriended her years ago, and look. Never really got anywhere in the business, and died with a big joke on his face. Styles is hopping around on one leg, with people poisoning his liquor. A laughable figure. Where are the husbands of yesteryear? Gone and forgotten. I was on the way to stardom and I wound up playing a series of miserable heavies on TV westerns. The only reason I was hired for this opera is because I'm one of Carol's exes. It makes newspaper copy, and The Monster needs all he can get. Enjoy our Carol's romantic play and you wind up behind the eight ball. Have you had a chance to watch Mr. Francis X. Garrity very closely? He's shriveling up like a man dying of cancer. The Carol poison is in his blood. And you'll be next, Mark, unless you meant what you said—that you've had enough."

Fleming suddenly gripped the edges of the small round table, and his voice was low and shaken. "I'm going to say this once, Orrin," he said. "Just once. From the moment you came on this lot you've been sniping at Carol. Do you know why you're here? Because you'd had a run of bad luck. Because Carol is a kind, decent person. She made the suggestion to Monty that you'd be good for the role. It wasn't his idea. He warned her about the kind of publicity your being here would bring. She thought she could take it, and you got the job. You owe her something better than this kind of cheap talk. So lay off."

Pell laughed. "Maybe I've missed my cue," he said. "Maybe our Carol wanted me back after all. All this time I thought *you* had the inside track, Mark."

The table went over. Glasses smashed on the floor. Sherry Garth, a drink spilled on the skirt of her dinner dress, stood up with a little scream. Fleming had Pell by the front of his jacket with his left hand. His right struck a pile-driving blow squarely on Pell's mouth. The dark actor went over backwards in his chair and fell heavily to the floor. Fleming was on his feet, standing over him.

Pell struggled up, hand pressed against his mouth. When he took the hand away, blood ran down on his chin. "You fool," he said in a foolishly bewildered voice, "you've broken my tooth."

Fleming hit him again, and he went down to his knees.

"Mark, stop it!" Sherry cried out.

It had all happened so fast that only then did the crowd close in. Two or three of the men grabbed Fleming. He made no effort to break free.

Pell struggled slowly to his feet. There were tears of

anger in his eyes. "I'll settle with you later for this, Fleming," he said. He turned and walked unsteadily out of the room.

A camera flash bulb set eyes to blinking. Then another. Fleming, ash-gray, looked angrily around at the flushed, excited faces. Then, with a kind of violent shudder, he shook himself free from the men who'd grabbed him by the arms.

"I want to make a speech to all you bastards," he said in a hard, cold voice. "You punks are responsible for everything that's happened here. You who call yourselves reporters—you're nothing but a bunch of psychotic keyhole peepers. You never look at any of us as human beings. We're great big glittering symbols of all the rotten things you'd like to be yourselves. Peter Styles is right. *You* make the climate that we live in. *You've* destroyed all the old codes of morality, not us! *You* feed the public on gossip and half-truths. And the tensions grow and grow until something gives way. An old woman was killed here because a climate for killing had been created by *you.*" He drew a deep breath. "There isn't one of you standing there drooling at me who'd believe me if I told you that I'm in love with Carol Richmond but that nothing—*nothing*—has gone on between us. Nothing but words! It wouldn't suit you to believe it. You wouldn't be able to hint at something else, laugh behind your hands at us, conjure up lewd pictures in your stinking little minds. Well, I've stopped smiling at you and playing the big star for you. From now on I'm going to treat slander as slander should be treated. Any one of you gossips about us, in print or in private, and I know it—I'll take pleasure in breaking your goddamned necks!"

He turned on his heel and walked quickly out through the French doors at the end of the room and into the night.

Francis X. Garrity seemed to have shrunk inside his clothes. He sat huddled in the armchair in his room, eyes blank with horror, staring at Jacobs, Peter and Sergeant Tresh, who stood in a little semicircle in front of him. He moistened dry, cracked-looking lips.

"You're suggesting that I—I killed Mrs. Moffet?" he whispered.

"I suggest it," Jacobs said grimly. "I suggest you went up to your rooms after you'd picked up your mail this morning and found her there. What had she discovered? Where you'd hidden the stolen makeup kit? Had she found the knife or the razor with which you'd cut the saddle girth?"

"My God!" Garrity said.

"Look in the bathroom, Sergeant," Jacobs said. Tresh took off. "We've learned a good deal about your insane jealousy of your wife, Garrity. You were prepared to do almost anything to break up what was going on here, break up her career, get her to yourself."

"No! I could wait! I was ready to wait!"

"You called the men in her life 'clowns,' didn't you? It was your phrase for them, wasn't it?" Peter asked.

"I may have—"

"You found Barton after his accident," Jacobs said. "You painted his face. You had the equipment, didn't you, in that stolen makeup kit?"

"No!"

"You drugged my drink," Peter said, "and then came into my room last night when I'd passed out and painted my face too."

"No! What are you talking about!"

"Your private way of exposing the enemy!" Jacobs said.

Tresh came back from the bathroom. He was carrying a black lacquer box. In it were two old-fashioned straight razors. The sergeant took one of them out of the box and showed it to Jacobs. "My father used to have a set like this," Tresh said. "This one—recently honed and sharpened, but there's a big nick in it."

"Leather is tougher than whiskers!" Jacobs said. "All right, Mr. Garrity, let's get to the truth. You cut that saddle girth with this razor. You meant to do in Fleming, but unfortunately for you Fleming and your wife switched saddles. No wonder you didn't want to bring the police into the picture. A proper investigation might have led to you."

"I swear—"

"Is this what Mrs. Moffet found?" Jacobs demanded, holding out the razor. "She was interested in trying to find out the truth about that saddle girth incident because two of the boys who worked for her were under suspicion. Did she confront you with it? Is that why you grabbed the candlestick and went to work on her?"

Garrity opened his mouth like an out-of-water fish gasping for air. Then his eyes seemed to roll up into his head and, very slowly, he toppled out of the chair and onto the rug.

"I think this is it," Jacobs said quietly. He wiped little beads of sweat from his forehead with his handkerchief. "See if you can scare up Doc Graham, Sergeant."

Peter looked down at the twisted face of the man sprawled out on the rug, frowning. "It looks like a stroke," he said. "He may not do any more talking for a long time. We'd better move him to the bed."

It seemed to be over.

Jacobs stayed in Garrity's room to wait for the doctor. There was a chance Garrity might speak—say something more. Peter went down the hall to the door of Carol's room where Trooper Childers stood guard. Carol should be told that at least the major heat was off. But Childers, politely, refused to let Peter go into the room.

"Not without Ben Jacobs gives his okay, Mr. Styles."

"Is Mrs. Howard in there with her?" Peter asked.

"Yeah."

"You could pass on a message from me," Peter said. "Have Mrs. Howard tell her I said to relax. Jacobs thinks he's found the real answer."

Peter found himself thinking of Mark Fleming. The news would be important to him. Peter started down the stairs to look for the actor. The party in the dining room was in full swing. Louis Armstrong's unique, husky voice rose above the laughing voices in a beat version of "Hello, Dolly." Peter was just approaching the door to the dining room when Sherry Garth came out. The front of her dress had a dark, wet stain on it.

"Spilled drink," she said. "You missed the excitement, Peter." She gave him a brief account of the row between Mark and Orrin Pell.

"But you look as though you had news," she said.

"Carol may be in the clear," Peter said. "It begins to shape up in Francis Garrity's direction."

Sherry's face brightened for an instant and then she made an angry little gesture. "I hate myself," she said. "Orrin's right. The first thing I thought of was 'the picture can go on.' God, we are a pack of heels, Peter. Are you going to tell Monty? It will take him off his particular hot seat."

"I was looking for Mark. I thought it might ease some of his anxiety. I don't particularly care whether The Monster suffers a little longer or not."

"Mark went outside," Sherry said. "He needed cooling off, I guess."

Peter avoided the dining room. If he showed himself there, he'd be buried under questions. He slipped into the deserted library and went out through its French doors onto the terrace.

The night was dark. There should have been a moon, but it was hidden behind dark clouds. Lights from the house illuminated the terrace to a degree, but a few yards out, the lawns were dark and impenetrable.

There was no sign of Mark on the terrace itself. Peter called his name. There was no answer. He walked out beyond the perimeter of light from the house, into the darkness, calling Mark's name again. Dark shadows of shrubbery dotted the lawn and faded away into complete blackness.

And then Peter heard someone running.

"Mark!

There was no answer. And then the running person crashed into a bush in the darkness. There was a smothered oath—a man's voice. Then complete silence.

"Mark!"

Peter moved in the direction of the runner.

"I've got good news for you, Mark. Don't hide out on me, fella."

And then he stumbled heavily and nearly fell. On his hands and knees he reached out to feel for what had tripped him—and his hands touched a body. Even that close, he couldn't see who it was. Had the runner knocked himself out as he crashed into a bush or tree?

Peter fumbled in his pocket for his lighter. The small flame burned still and straight in the darkness.

Stretched out on the damp grass was Mark Fleming. And as Peter held the light closer, he felt the small hairs rise on the back of his head. Mark's face, turned to one side, was white—white with the makeup used on clowns. The mask hadn't been completed, but the basic white was there.

"Mark!"

Peter tried to move him, and instantly drew back his hand. It was wet and red. There was an ugly wound at the back of the man's head. He was breathing, but he was out cold.

Then an old, almost forgotten instinct took charge of Peter. It had been developed long ago on the dark Korean mountainsides. He rolled away from Mark's body just in time to miss a blow aimed at him from behind. A hard-breathing figure stumbled over Mark and plunged down onto the grass a few yards away.

The lighter was out.

The only sound was the heavy breathing of the attacker.

5

In the total darkness, Peter moved, slowly, tentatively, trying to get his good leg under him so that he could rise without sound. And even as he struggled up, muscles tensed, he knew that everything was all wrong. Whoever was over there in the dark, trying to control his breathing so that he could hear Peter, it was not Francis Garrity. It was not Francis Garrity who had slugged Mark and started to paint on the clown face.

From the direction of the house the hi-fi blared. There was very little chance of attracting attention by calling for help. In the darkness there was no way to tell what the attacker was armed with. The blow on the back of Mark's head could have been made with a gun butt. In terms of a personal fight with the unknown man, tactics would have called for Peter to slip back toward the circle of light outside the house, where he could see who he was fighting and how to fight him. But he hesitated to move away from where Mark lay. The other man might take the opportunity to finish Mark off.

Peter strained to hear something. The man had caught his breath now, and there wasn't a sound from anywhere.

"Hello, Dolly!" Louis Armstrong's voice drifted out into the blackness.

Peter bent down, feeling along the grass for something he could pick up and throw. If he could trick his man into moving— But Clarissa Moffet's ground crew kept the lawns as clean of broken branches or stones as a vacuumed rug. And then, as Peter still crept softly across the grass, feeling for something, a hand touched his face.

Peter darted back, straightening up, and caught a wild swinging fist on the side of his jaw. It staggered him. An angry, growling sound came from the attacker. Another blow just grazed Peter's chin, and then Peter, his jaw tucked in, bored in. He took another savage blow, this one off the top of his head, and then he closed with the other man. He locked his arms around the man, pinioning him. The growl grew to a kind of roar. A hot, alcoholic breath almost choked Peter. The man swung Peter from side to side, but he couldn't break the hold that was slowly bending him back. The man was very strong, wiry.

For a moment Peter thought he had him, and then the man butted Peter in the face with the top of his head. Stars went off in front of Peter's eyes. His hold on the man was broken as he staggered back. A knee came up and caught him in the stomach, the toe of a shoe smashed into his shin. It would have been crippling, but it caught him on his plastic leg and not the good one. But it knocked him down. He rolled away, covering his head with his arms. That gun butt, or whatever it was, could finish him now.

But the man ran.

Peter scrambled up, fiery little dots still dancing in front of his eyes. He couldn't tell which way the man had gone, but he stared hard at the house and the circle of light. If the man ran through it, there just might be a chance of identifying him.

There was no sign of him.

Peter took his lighter out of his pocket again and located Mark by its flame. The wound at the back of the actor's head was bleeding profusely.

Peter put his hands under the actor's armpits and began to drag him as gently as he could toward the circle of light. Peter was drenched with sweat, and his face and head felt as if he'd been beaten with clubs. It was only a few yards, but it seemed like miles before he dragged Mark onto the terrace and onto the circle of light. He looked around, hesitating, and saw no one. Then he ran with his curious skipping run to the French doors opening into the dining room.

Noise billowed out at him as he wrenched one of the doors open. He was in luck. Standing right by the door and talking to one of the girls in the company was Bill Tompkins.

"What in hell's happened to you?" Bill said.

Peter glanced down and saw that his clothes were smeared with grass stains. There was blood on his hand, and he knew his mouth was badly swollen at one corner.

"Out here, quick," Peter said.

The girl came with Bill. Peter heard a little gasp from her as she saw Mark sprawled out on the flagstones.

"You had a fight with him?" Bill said, not believing it.

"A killer's on the loose," Peter said. "I had a fight with him, not Mark. They sent for a doctor to take care of Garrity. Go upstairs and see if he's come. Mark's badly hurt."

"I'll go," the girl said, and she ran toward the house.

"And bring Ben Jacobs," Peter called after her.

"What's happened to his face?" Bill said.

"I interrupted an artist at work," Peter said bitterly. "Another clown face in the making. I fought with the sonofabitch, but I never even got a glimpse of him. All I know is he'd been drinking."

"Pell," Bill suggested. "I had a feeling he'd be gunning for Fleming."

"Maybe," Peter said. He lifted exploring fingers to his tender jaw. "Got a head like a rock!" He knelt beside Mark. "Lucky if it's no worse than a concussion. The base of his skull could be smashed in."

People began flooding out of the dining room now. The girl had evidently passed the word on her way to find Jacobs and the doctor. At the same moment a couple of troopers came running around the corner of the house.

"You see anyone go into the house the front way?" Peter asked the troopers.

"No. No one went in the front door. We were stationed there. What happened here?"

"Take care of him," Peter said, not answering the question. He started for the house. A reporter tugged at his sleeve, but Peter shook himself free. Just inside the dining room door, he met Jacobs and Dr. Graham coming out.

"You're needed out there," Peter told Dr. Graham. Then he quickly told the scowling Jacobs his story. "He ran in the direction of the house. There are twenty ways he could get in. The troopers on the front door say he didn't go that way."

"This blows us sky-high," Jacobs said angrily. "Why would he come into the house? We can catch him here."

"I don't think I marked him," Peter said. "I didn't have a chance. If he runs, you've got him. If he has a moment or two to clean up and calm down in here, how do we finger him?"

A huge figure came at them from the inside hall. "This has got to stop!" Monty Spain bellowed. "Is my whole damn company going to be destroyed while you stand around here twiddling your thumbs?"

Jacobs ignored him. "We'll do a quick search of the

house," Jacobs said. "I've got eight or ten men here. Maybe we can catch him changing. He must have grass stains on his clothes like you have, Styles."

Jacobs ran out onto the terrace.

Monty Spain raised a massive fist and looked up at the ceiling. "You cut it out!" he shouted. "I've had enough of this."

Peter almost laughed. The Monster was actually threatening God! Then, in a completely conversational tone, he asked Peter how badly Fleming was hurt.

Peter never got a chance to answer that question.

There was a thundering roar and the whole house shook as if it had been struck by a bomb. Monty Spain staggered back against the wall. Peter, lurching into a table, heard the sound of shattering glass.

Outside on the terrace women screamed.

Peter choked on the pungent smell of oil smoke.

Then from outside came the cry of *"Fire!"*

Peter's first thought was of Carol. He turned and ran as quickly as his leg allowed him up the stairway to the second floor. Someone raced past him going in the same direction. It was Buck Marshall, wearing his white houseman's coat and his black glasses. At the head of the stair, Peter saw Buck head into Francis Garrity's room.

Carol and Mrs. Howard were already at the door of their room.

"Out quick!" Peter said. "I think the oil burner blew."

Black clouds of choking oil smoke drifted up the stairwell and set them all to coughing. Peter put his arm around Carol and started toward the main stairway with her. The smoke drove them back, hot and thick.

Then Buck came out of the next room, carrying the limp Garrity in his arms. "Back stair!" he shouted. "It's enclosed.

May be clear."

Excited shouting voices drifted up with the thick smoke. Peter found the back stair and opened the door to them. The air was clear. He stood aside to let Buck go first with his burden, and then he, Carol and Mrs. Howard followed. Peter closed the door behind them. For a moment they stood there, gasping in reasonably fresh air. But the smoke began to sift through to them under the bottom of the hall door.

They hurried down into the kitchen, out the back door and onto the lawn. Peter found himself standing there, his arms around Carol, looking back at the house. Smoke poured out of cellar windows and some of the windows on the ground floor. But Peter saw no flames.

Buck had put Garrity down on the grass. He was breathing hard. He took off the white jacket and covered Garrity with it.

"There's a real fancy sprinkler system in the basement," he said to Peter. "Should control it some. It was the oil burner, all right. Firebox fills with oil without the motor starting—then it does, and boom!"

Carol's warm body was pressed tightly against Peter, and she was crying softly. "I don't think I can stand anything more, Peter. Not anything more."

He didn't tell her about Mark. That might be one too many. He told himself, bitterly, that this confusion had played straight into the killer's hands. Grass stains or blood or any other evidences of the attack on Mark and the struggle with Peter could be explained away on the grounds of escape from the house. Broken glass could account for cuts. A fall as he ran out of the house would explain grass stains or torn clothing.

"How bad is Fleming?" Buck asked.

Peter swore softly under his breath. He felt Carol stiffen

in his arms.

"What's wrong with Mark?" she asked.

"Someone slugged him out on the lawn," Peter said. "I interrupted another face-painting job."

"Oh, God!"

"He's all right. He's out of the house. Dr. Graham's with him."

"But it couldn't have been Francis!" Carol said, eyes turning toward the still figure on the grass covered by Buck's white coat.

"It couldn't have been Francis," Peter said.

"What's wrong with him, Peter?"

"He collapsed while Jacobs was questioning him," Peter said. "I'm afraid it was a stroke."

"Bad one, according to the Doc," Buck said. His voice turned angry. "Sonsofbitches! Did they really think he was the killer? Francis wouldn't hurt a fly!"

"I've got to go to Mark," Carol said.

Peter held her firmly. "We'd better stay put here."

From far away he heard the distant wail of a fire siren.

"You don't know who it was, Peter?" Carol asked.

"No," he said. "It was pitch-dark. I struggled with him but he got away."

"Anyone checked on Pell?" Buck asked. "He was boiling after the fight. I saw him."

And so it was necessary to tell Carol the whole bit.

"It's always me! It's always me that makes the trouble!" she said.

Just then Jacobs, a handkerchief held to his face, came staggering out the front door of the house. As his eyes grew accustomed to the dim light, he saw the little group on the lawn.

"Everyone okay?" he asked.

"By luck," Buck said. "The back stair was clear of

smoke."

"The fire's out," Jacobs said. "Sprinkler system. Never had much faith in them, but this one worked efficiently."

A blinking red light, accompanied by a screaming siren, came up the driveway. The local chemical truck had arrived. Other fire equipment was following it up from the stone gates.

"Fierce smoke damage downstairs," Jacobs said. "God, all those paintings and antiques. Some of them ruined. The rest will take months to restore."

"And our man is swallowed up in the excitement," Peter said. "If he'd managed it on purpose, it couldn't have worked better for him."

"Maybe he did," Jacobs said, mopping at his face. "Oil cock opened in the basement. Oil ran all over the floor. Then someone turned the thermostat on full at the head of the cellar stairs and it all went off with a bang. It could have been done on purpose."

"I want to get away from here. I never want to see Marlingham again," Carol cried out. "Where's Mark?"

Jacobs ignored her. "There's an ambulance with that fire equipment, Marshall," he said. "Both Garrity and Fleming should be taken to the hospital. See if you can get the driver and his man here with the stretcher."

Buck raced off across the lawn toward the fire trucks and the ambulance.

"Nobody else will leave here till we get to the bottom of this," Jacobs said, as if giving a delayed answer to Carol. "First thing we do is get everybody together and count heads. Terrace seems to be the best place until we get the smoke cleared out of the house. You'll all come round there, please. Mrs. Howard, please bring Miss Richmond. Styles, keep an eye on Garrity till they get him to the ambulance, will you? Then join us."

"I'll need some kind of wrap," Carol said, still clinging to Peter. "It's cold."

"Mrs. Howard will find something for you in the house," Jacobs said. "I make you responsible for Miss Richmond, Styles." He walked briskly away toward the corner of the house, followed by Mrs. Howard.

"Peter," Carol said, like a small child crying for help. Her face was buried against Peter's chest. He felt the strange excitement of years ago—the moment of first love. He wanted to protect her. He wanted to hold her. Could it be that out of all this was to come a new direction in his own life?

"I should go with Francis, shouldn't I?" Carol said. "It's the least I could do for him."

"He wouldn't know if you were there or not," Peter said. He glanced down at Garrity. There was a faint rattling sound in the man's throat as he struggled weakly for breath. Francis X. Garrity was never going to realize his dream of a quiet retirement with his glamorous wife.

Two men came across the lawn with a stretcher. Buck Marshall wasn't one of them. Carol kept her face turned away as the men lifted Garrity onto the stretcher and carried him toward the ambulance.

"I did this to him," Carol whispered. "I did it by letting him come into my life at all. Stay away from me, Peter. Knowing me is poison!"

"Don't be an idiot," Peter said quietly.

"Oh, Peter!"

The mood was broken by the sound of Buck Marshall's voice, high and shrill. It came from some distance away near a clump of lilac bushes."

"Hey, Pete! Look what I found!"

Buck came into view in the rim of light from the house. He wasn't alone. He was walking behind a dark, struggling figure. Peter saw that Buck had the man's arm twisted behind him. As they came closer, Peter saw that it was Orrin Pell.

"This baby was trying to sneak away in the excitement," Buck said. His smile glittered white and angry. The lights from the house reflected in little orange dots on his black glasses. Pell, his mouth swollen and bruised, protested loudly.

"I was just trying to get away from the fire, you damn fool!" he said. "What are you trying to do, break my arm. Call off your dog, will you, Carol?"

Buck gave Pell a little shove toward Peter and Carol and then came quickly up behind him and began to pat over his clothes. "Hey, what have we here?" He reached into the side pocket of Pell's jacket and brought out something in his hand. He held it up in the faint light. It was a small, compact automatic. Pell stared at it, his face twitching.

"And what else?" Buck said cheerfully. Once more he searched the actor's pockets. He produced a pipe, a lighter, and something else which Peter didn't instantly recognize.

"Tube of grease paint!" Buck said, his excitement rising. "White grease paint! Watch him, Pete!" Buck snapped on the lighter and held the flame close to the tube. " 'Schwall and McIntyre,' " he read from the label. "That's the outfit that makes your special stuff, isn't it, Carol?"

Carol was staring at Pell, her eyes wide. "Orrin!" she said in a shocked voice.

"I never saw those things before in my life!" Pell cried. "What kind of a frame-up is this?"

"That's the way it always goes, isn't it?" Buck said. "Frame-up! Hah! This is our boy, Pete. The one who painted Barton's face, and yours, and Mark's, and murdered the old lady. I guess this is the gun he slugged Mark with."

Peter stood very still, his arm firmly around a shaking Carol, "Let me see the gun, Buck," he said quietly.

"A .32 Police Special," Buck said. "I should have figured you from the start, Pell. Couldn't stand being around Carol again, could you? Had to make clowns out of all her boy friends. Tried to frame Francis too, didn't you? What happened? The old lady find you trying to put the razor back in Francis' case? That why you slugged her?"

"This guy is out of his mind!" Pell said. He sounded frightened.

"Let me have a look at the gun, Buck," Peter said.

"Regular police special," Buck said. He made no move to pass it to Peter.

Peter took Carol's shoulders in his hands and moved her so that she was standing behind him. "How did you know, Buck, that he painted my face?" he asked. "I didn't tell you. You didn't see it—or did you?"

"Sure I did, Pete. Came in last night to see how you were."

"You didn't mention it to me."

Buck laughed. "You didn't mention it to *me,*" he said "Figured if you didn't want to talk about it, I wouldn't talk about it."

"Considerate of you," Peter said in a cold voice. "Carol, go to the terrace and get Jacobs. Tell him to bring a couple of troopers. Tell him it's all over. I've got his man."

"I'll say we got him," Buck said. "Cold—with the goods on him."

"Go!" Pete said to Carol.

Buck took a step backward. Something that was meant to be a laugh came from him. "I wish Francis could know I nailed this bastard. I would do anything in the world for Francis."

"Let's stop kidding around, shall we, Buck? *Will you*

please go, Carol!"

The Police Special was suddenly fitted comfortably into the palm of Buck Marshall's right hand. It was leveled straight at Peter.

"I don't like jokers!" he said.

"Odd from a man who's been thriving on miserable jokes for a long time," Peter said, level, cold. "Sooner or later everyone had to have alibis for some part of this thing except the guilty person. You told me about it awhile ago, only I wouldn't listen. You wanted Carol, only she wouldn't have you. And so you decided to get even with her and with Francis and with everybody else who had anything to do with her. I guess you just told us what happened with Mrs. Moffet. She caught you putting the razor back in Francis' case. Why did you wait so long to return it, Buck? The girth was cut over a week ago."

"Because—" The white smile was pasted on his face, and little rivulets of sweat ran down his forehead. "Okay, wise guy," he said. "You're asking for it." The knuckles showed white on his gun hand.

And then, before Peter could stop her, Carol walked around him and straight toward Buck, directly in the line of fire.

"There's been enough trouble, Buck," she said. "If you want me to go with you, I will."

"It's too late, baby," Buck said. "Too damned late. You had your chance to stop all this, and you wouldn't do it. I wasn't good enough for you, was I? I didn't have Francis' dough, or all the fake good manners of a Rex Barton, or a Styles, or the publicity value of a Pell or a Fleming. You're a fake. You weren't ever interested in love or sex—you wanted dough, and your name in the papers linked up with the right guy so they'd make you more and more dough. You didn't want a man! A man who could make you forget you were anything but a woman. If you were really a woman, you'd have forgotten all about the movie crap and the glamor crap. You are and always were a fake."

"It's not too late!" Carol said in a clear, high voice.

"Sure it is, baby. Because I don't want you any more. I thought I had you wrapped up good with the old lady's murder. Except for this nosy Styles bastard, I would have had you. It would have been fun to watch you die slow, with the paint stripped off you, and the glamor stripped off you. It would have been the pay-off for me and maybe dozens of other real guys you gave the brush to. Well, it's going to have to be quick, baby, because whatever happens to me, you aren't going to go on playing games. I got to make this all worth my while, you see? So beg me once more. I'd like you to beg me once more."

Out of the corner of his eye Peter saw that Pell had backed away. He was going to be no help. The distance between Buck and himself was far too great to make before the finger on the trigger squeezed tight. And Carol would get it first. But you couldn't just stand here and be mowed down.

Peter dove forward. The force of his plunge caught Carol back of the knees and she went down. Peter rolled over on top of her, shielding her body with his own.

The gun went off—two, three, four times.

You couldn't be shot and not feel it, Peter thought. There was no jolting, seering pain of bullets in his back. His face was against Carol's.

"My God, my God!" she was saying in a whispered sob.

Peter turned his head.

Buck Marshall was down on his knees, hands clutching at his stomach. Blood sifted through his clawing fingers. The gun lay beside him, but Buck made no move to pick it up. His face was twisted into a grimace of mortal agony.

Peter sprang to his feet. Then he saw the explanation. Mrs. Howard, the policewoman, stood a few yards away, her face dead white, staring almost stupidly at a smoking gun in her hand. The wrap she'd brought for Carol lay on the grass at her feet. She looked up at Peter slowly.

"I—I never fired at anything but a target before," she said. "I—I almost c-couldn't pull the trigger."

"It is part of the crazy pattern of our times," Ben Jacobs said to Peter some hours later in the smoke-damaged library at Marlingham. "Cops are our enemies. The laws of the land are meant for somebody else, not us. Jim Walters, the ground crew fellow, helped me put it together."

Peter was only half listening. His muscles ached. Those few brief moments of frozen tension while Carol stood between him and Buck Marshall's ravings, between him and that menacing gun, had stretched him physically almost beyond endurance. The fear of making the wrong move or no move at all before it was too late had been like being stretched on a rack. After the climax moment, it still seemed like a distorted nightmare. He remembered Jacobs and others running toward them across the lawn. He remembered picking Carol up and holding her close. He remembered hearing Orrin Pell explaining what had happened, making it sound as though he had had some heroic part in the finish. He remembered thinking, for one almost delirious moment, that the world had come full circle for him—from that day when he'd held a fourteen-year-old girl in his arms on the bank of a New England trout stream to the present, when he held the woman she'd become, her cheek pressed against his, whispering his name. He remembered the absurd sound of Monty Spain's booming voice saying: "*Now* what?" And then he remembered being alone. Dr. Graham had told Carol that Mark Fleming was not as badly hurt as they'd feared. He was in his room on the second floor at Marlingham. He could see her. Peter remembered Carol's soft voice. "Dear Peter, how can I ever thank you?" And she was gone to find Mark. The daydream of a romantic ending to twenty-four hours of horror drifted away. Francis Garrity had died on the way to the hospital. Carol was free to make her choice, and she'd made it.

Buck Marshall would die in a matter of hours without, the doctors informed Jacobs, ever making a statement. Mrs. Howard's target practice had made her grimly efficient —for which, Peter told himself, thank God.

"Walters knew something?" Peter heard himself ask.

"The movie people—they didn't want the cops in on that saddle girth incident. It would be bad publicity," Jacobs said. He said it with a kind of contemptuous anger. "And Clarissa Moffet? She was trying to save some remnants of Marlingham's name and fame. She decided to do her own investigating—to save the boys who worked for her. The day after the accident, they found that old-fashioned razor hidden away behind one of the feed bins in the stable. The nick in it told them, when they compared it with jagged cuts on the girth, that it had been used to cut the strap. Did they promptly report it? They did not! They live in the New World—the world of every man for himself. Mrs. Moffet had a purpose now when she wandered through the house. Who had owned that razor? She found out soon enough that it belonged to Francis Garrity. But had Garrity used it—or was it Carol or Buck Marshall who had easy access to it—or almost anyone else? If it was Garrity, why had he left it to be found? It could have been easily traced to him. So they did nothing, waiting to see what would happen.

"Then this morning Eddie Teliskie, one of the stable-boys, saw Marshall sneak into the barn and remove the razor from its hiding place. Did he grab him? He did not. Did he tell Walters? He did not. He called the big house on the phone and got Mrs. Moffet, who was distributing flowers. And so this courageous but stupid old lady went up to the Garrity suite and waited, and—here we guess—Marshall appeared with the razor, to replace it in the case. She confronted him—and that was that."

"But why would he return it—after a week?" Peter asked.

"Hard to put yourself inside that twisted mind," Jacobs said. "He was out to nail everybody; to make fools of Carol's men friends, to destroy Francis Garrity whom he pretended to love and admire. The men in Carol's life. Who knows what got him going, but he was going full speed. When nobody found the razor in the barn, I can only guess he decided to speed things up. He would return it to the case. Then, blandly, in front of witnesses, he would show the nicked razor to Garrity—hinting around so that it would become quite clear that Garrity was the villain of the saddle girth. After that, he ran wild."

"You think he started the fire?"

"Who else? How else? You'd nearly caught him working over Mark. The confusion would give him time to cover his tracks. Of course he blew the whole game when he tried to pin it on Pell, planting the gun and the grease paint on him right there in front of you. You know, Styles, you could do me a favor."

"What?"

"When you write your piece, ram it down their throats that we can't make our own private worlds to live in. We have to live in the same world with everyone else, and by the same laws as everyone else. We can't make our own rules or invent our own moralities."

Ah, yes, there was a piece to write.